# Love by Any Other Name

## SHORT ROMANTIC TALES

### REI ROSENQUIST

# Ready to Fly

a short romance

## Rei Rosenquist

*For K*
*In loving memory*

*January 2014 ~ January 2023*

Seattle

I get off my flight and step out of the canned air of Paradise Left Behind into the fresh, damp, cold world I know so well. The touristy trappings of Hawai'i fall away as I leave the gate behind: hibiscus flowers, pictures of beach sunsets, pineapples in boxes, the fake smell of coconut sunscreen. I press my way through the throngs of Bermuda shorts, floral print shirts, and seasonally inappropriate sandals bought at the convenience store.

The Seattle-Tacoma airport rises up around me like thin familiar arms: rain drenched, gray, and chilly. Just the way I like things. I happily tug my tweed sweater from my small purple rolley carry-on covered in cheesy Hawaiian flowers, the name of which I keep forgetting. Hibiscus maybe? No, something with a "p." But not poinsettias; those are winter plants and don't come from the tropics at all, despite appearances. I think. Plants aren't my strong suit. I'll have to ask Mariza when she arrives to pick me up.

I carry on through the terminal, straightening my hair with my fingers trying to look less island-swept and more sharp, sleek city professional. My silky black hair tangles easily between my fingers as I straighten my side-part. I have my grandfather to thank for this hair. And these long thin fingers. Sushi-making fingers, my dad -- Otousan -- says. I've never made a maki roll in my entire life, but he assures me I could move back to Okinawa, Japan where dad's family came from and open a shop of my own.

But, I'm happy enough where I am. I love studying insects, and Seattle isn't so bad I need to up and leave right now. Sure, it's grayer than I'd like and the cold sinks into my tropical bones, but I've come to terms with it. Layers, that's the key. Tank top, button down, vest, hoodie, and a blazer. Skinny jeans with a wrap-around skirt. Not only do layers keep my tiny frame warm, but they make for lots of interesting non-binary combinations.

Pausing in the middle of the causeway to pull my Seattle-grey sweater over my head, I get a strong whiff of sea-salted air and a light masculine cologne.

In a whirlwind of emotion, I'm whisked back across the ocean, back to O'ahu, back to the long golden beach of Kailua as its drenched in orange and red sunset light.

A pearly white crescent moon overhead warned of the coming end of a phase, but I paid it no mind. Kai and I strolled the beach lackadaisically, arm in arm, as if we had nowhere else in the universe to go, nothing more to do but admire the sky's colorful light display.

Another perfect tropical dusk.

With Kai's hand in mine, I let myself dream wildly. I considered staying in Hawai'i for good. Dreamed of getting the perfect job at the conservatory. Dreamed of Maritza joining me with our little flock of birds. Dreamed of a huge outdoor aviary the birds could enjoy year-round. Dreamed of Mariza meeting Kai and hitting it off.

Then, my phone jangled against my hip. I checked the screen and saw an email saying the position at the nature research institute had been filled. And then, right on top of it, I received a call from my veterinarian in Washington telling me that Koko -- the timid green cheeked conure who Maritza, my partner, and I had rescued together -- had fallen ill yet again.

And I knew right then, in a bright green flash of still-damaged wings, that I had to go home. That my dream had been just that -- wild fantasy.

My hand fell from Kai's as I hung up the phone. Overhead, dark ominous storm clouds rolled in. Kai looked up with a new expression I hadn't seen before. His dark mysterious eyes studied the sky like a writer might study a problematic sentence in a first draft. Expertly trained, looking for patterns no one else would see.

"Rain will be on us in about five minutes," he said without doubt.

I wondered, then, what Kai did for a living. Was he a navigator on the sea? Did he work for one of the multitude of shipping companies around Hawai'i? Was he a professional pilot or one in training? He'd never mentioned planes or boats to me, but then we never talked about anything so mundane. We talked about philosophy and enjoyed the world together.

But, I was leaving soon, and I felt a sudden burning need to know. I struggled with forming a question that wouldn't sound ridiculously out of place, but his voice interrupted me before I could find the right wording.

"That's going to be one big blessing from the sky coming our way," he said with a chuckle.

"I don't personally believe in that," I replied in a sad way.

I'd never been a spiritual person myself. Never believed in gods or blessings from beings I couldn't engage with. I was a scientist, after all. Tangible proof was my first tongue, and I'd spoken it all my life.

Kai smiled at me, somewhat slyly. "What's there not to believe in? Rain brings water to the ground, and we all need water to grow."

I smiled back because I understood that he was trying to comfort me. And while the phrase still sounded spiritual, he had meant it in a practical way that my scientific brain could accept.

"Thank you," I said, full of gratitude.

"You just got bad news," Kai said wisely.

"Yes, I have to leave O'ahu as soon as possible."

I'll never forget the way Kai hugged me, then. Big and warm. Like the ground underneath our feet could crumble and fall away, but somehow, magically, we'd still remain standing. So long as I was in Kai's arms, I was safe and sound.

I didn't believe that, either, but it was a nice dream.

We let go and walked the rest of the beach in a strange, unfamiliar silence. When we got to our cars, we touched foreheads. Kai pressed his nose against mine and breathed in. I breathed in a moment too late, and by the time I exhaled my half of our shared breath, the rain was coming down just as hard as Kai had promised. Whatever words we might have said were swallowed by the roaring sound. Behind us, the tumbling hiss of the tossing ocean mixed with the crackling rattle of bent palm trees, and the sound made for a sharp and cold farewell.

The doors to baggage claim open and slap me in the face, almost as cold as wind that day.

I shiver and try to get my bearings, dragging my rolley bag to a stop. Which carousel did the flight attendant say again? B? I look around for signs, oddly out of place in my home airport, frazzled and saddened by the memories of that storm, Kai, and the sun setting on my life in Hawai'i.

"Excuse me," someone says behind me, trying to get around the obstruction to traffic I've become standing in the middle of the walk way.

"Sorry," I say and step out of the way.

I get moving again, breathing in the coffee-scented air, and head toward baggage claim B on a whim. When I get there, the bags are already tumbling down the conveyor belt. I purchased a goofy hot pink and blue Hawaiian print match-set for just this moment. Easy spotting. I stand at the back of the crowd and wait.

Cold air slaps me in while I wait; each gust a reminder that I'm not in the tropics anymore. I straighten my Seattle gray sweater hiding the ocean-colored floral print tank top underneath. Homesickness rises up from nowhere like the scent of petunias.

No, that's not right. Something else with a "p." Pansies? No. Definitely need to ask Mariza. She'll know beyond a doubt.

I wasn't in Hawaii to study the flowers. I'm an entomologist, and I was in Hawai'i to study the plight of the local pollinators. I don't even know why the name of a flower is bothering me. A flash of Kai's dark sun-kissed face, those big black eyes, that full-lipped smile full of the light of life.

"Every flower is a good memory," Kai said when he gave me my parting gift -- a lei he'd hand made. He was full of that kind of wisdom he bore: metaphorical and intuitive. Big tall stories that struggled to hold their weight under the gaze of a Westernized world. Even if I hadn't always shared his belief-system, I'd loved hearing his perspective.

If only I'd said something in those last moments. A confession of being polyamorous, a wish to stay connected, even a vague hope for the future. Anything. But no. I'd let his hand slip from mine in a quietude I hadn't felt inside. Maybe he did -- feel peace and acceptance at my leaving so suddenly.

Maybe he won't even miss me.

I'll never know.

"Jun!"

I turn at the sound of my name, and there she is. Mariza. The first love of my life.

We're high school sweethearts; one of the two dating couples from our graduating class who made it last. We've been together for decades, and still every time I see her face -- it's fresh. A thrill of excitement shoots from my head to my toes, and my face breaks into a massive blushing grin.

I am so in love with this woman.

She's in my favorite autumn dress. It's black, covered in tiny red Japanese maple leaves that bring out the natural red highlights in her long thick black hair. She's let her bangs grow out again, just the way I like them, parted off to the left side. The deep black line across her face brings out her strong jawline, her regal high brow, and her rich mahogany eyes. Her full lips smile at me through my favorite deep maroon lipstick. Her curvy hips sway as she saunters toward me, already gushing in her rich, Spanish-accented voice. She wraps me in a huge bear hug, and I melt into her. Marizta is a balance of soft and strong.

De tal palo, tal astilla, I always say.

I'm beyond lucky to live in the presence of such strong women. My longing for Hawai'i fades away as Maritza combs my hair with her fingers, doting on every detail of my face.

"Mi amor. I'm so glad you made it back safe. Your flight was delayed. I've been worried sick. How was the trip? Did they feed you? Are you hungry? We can get something to eat. Do you need coffee? Ah. I've missed you so much."

Mariza pulls me into another hug and this time buries her face in my shoulder. I wrap my arms around her shoulders, holding her close against my heart. She smells like home. Flowers and their greenery mixed with a subtle warmth that's all her. I breathe the perfume in long and deep. She pulls away just enough to tilt her dark red lips toward mine and our kiss sweeps the clouds in my mind away. Her long black hair tumbles across my arms like a shower, and I'm utterly refreshed.

"I've missed you too," I say, breathless, when she pulls away.

"You look very tan," she gives me a fake glare. "Did you not get the sunscreen I sent? It was coral safe."

"I know, I know. I did use it, but you know how it goes. Long days in the field."

"And you forget to reapply. Some things never change."

She sounds spicy about my neglect, but when she sees my frown, she relents and grins. I know she's just teasing me, but I can't help feeling a little bruised. Likely, it's still the homesickness I'm trying to pretend isn't there. The longing for something gone.

I push that aside and kiss her. She nuzzles into the collar of my thick sweater. And for a moment, we just breathe together.

"It's good to be back," I say, and some part of me means it.

"It's good to have you," Maritza agrees.

"My bags!" I remember suddenly why we're still standing in the life-less baggage claim room surrounded by forgotten luggage and concrete.

"Got them right here. Hot pink and blue plumerias? Really?"

"Plumerias! That's it. I knew you'd recognize them. How'd you find my bags so quickly?"

"Hard to miss the giant "J" you drew with Koko perching in it."

I grin wide. "You noticed."

"Of course I noticed. And, I grabbed them all while you were off in la-la land."

My blush goes from pink to red. "Oh, yeah sorry about that."

"Let me guess, your local boy? What was his name again?"

"Kai, and yes. I was thinking about him."

"Well," Mariza puts a hand on her hip like she does when she's about to mock-lecture me. "You haven't given me all the juicy details, yet. I want to hear all about you and him!"

"I wish I had more to tell," I say, sighing.

Mariza loves hearing about my other love interests. It excites her knowing I'm happy, knowing I'm making someone else happy, knowing there is more love in the world than before. At my words, her face falls, genuinely sad.

"He wasn't available?" she asks.

I shrug, uncertain. "No, it's not that exactly. We were just friends, that's all. We took long walks on the beach. He invited me to dinner at his place once and we played dominoes by candle light."

"Sounds romantic," Mariza encourages, her grin returning. "Are you sure you weren't in denial?"

I shake my head. "I wasn't. We were companionable. Comfortable. Like old friends. We talked about philosophy and art theory, about society and culture. That's it."

"He didn't ask, you know, if you were interested?" Mariza asks, deflating in a shared gesture of disappointment.

"No. He's kind and gentle, but I never got the impression he was interested in love."

"Que pena," Mariza says, facing turning into a pout. "Too bad. I would have loved to move to Hawai'i for you and him."

"You don't even know him!" I tease, laughing because I know what she means.

She just wants me to be happy. I give her a big kiss. She returns my kiss, then pulls me away with a serious face. "I'm sorry he let you down."

"He didn't exactly *let me down*," I defend Kai. "It's not his fault. I never said anything."

"I'm still sad. For him. For you. For us. Love that sets sail without us hurts, regardless of why we miss the ship."

I can see the corners of her big beautiful eyes redden and dampen with tears. And I know she's remembering her own ship that set sail two years ago. A beautiful woman from Jamaica named Roma who worked on several projects with her. They hit it off, had loads of long talks. They took romantic walks in the park and cooked one another dinner once a week. Then, Roma's family member fell ill and that was that. She was on a flight back to Jamaica the next day. We've never heard from her again.

"Te amo. I love you," I say and kiss her more seriously.

"I love you too. I just want more people to see the you I do."

I look away, blushing and abashed. Her expression is so hopeful, so warm and bright, and it makes me wish even harder that I'd have said something to Kai. Because maybe she'd have been right. Maybe he would have been ready for love. Maybe he would have seen the full me and reciprocated.

"I just couldn't, you know, figure out how to talk to him about it? I don't even know if he'd have been game."

"For you? Are you kidding me?" Mariza gives me a playful slap on the butt. "You are one hot catch!"

"You know what I mean. I don't think he's queer, or poly, or even aware that there are different ways of being for that matter. He's kind of sheltered in a weird way. Or maybe just hyper-focused. He knows a lot about what he knows, but the rest of the world...well, it wasn't a conversation I ever figured out how to have. And then suddenly, with one day left to have it in? I just didn't think it was fair."

"Fair, bear, my big round derriere. Who ever said anything about love being fair?"

"It's better this way," I say, resting my head on her shoulder for a moment's worth of comfort. "It's not like we're ever going to see each other again, anyway."

"Si. You're probably right," Mariza says and sighs, resigning herself to my truth.

She gives my head a gentle scritch like we do when we want to tell our birds how much we love them. A few little rubs behind the ear. I nuzzle into her scritches for a moment, then pull away. "Let's get out of here. I could use some real coffee after that flight. How is Koko?"

We walk the rest of the way to the car catching up on Koko's health and the state of the rest of our flock. Nine birds in total, our house is a veritable bird sanctuary. In truth, it's an unofficial parrot rescue mission we never meant to have. But, once we rescued Koko, our eyes were opened. And then, one bird after another turned up on our radar, and we just couldn't say no.

We're both conservationists -- myself in the pollinators field and Mariza in the endangered plant rehabilitation field. And, while everyone and their auntie and uncle have heard about the cat and dog crisis in

America, how many people know about the unwanted and abused parrot crisis? Next to none.

So, all these birds are our family, yes, but they are also part of our job, which is our shared life passion. To rescue and preserve life when and where we can.

It's why I was in Hawaii for the spring and summer. It's why we live in the pacific northwest of America where there are lots of other activists and farmers to connect with. It's even how Mariza and I met. And it's what kept us together when polyamory went from being something interesting about us to something challenging that we had to really work though.

Being polyamorous is wonderful, but just like monogamy, it has it's road bumps and road blocks. Sometimes, things just go wrong. Being poly also poses the unique challenge of the mass majority of people not understanding that you aren't cheating, lying, or generally being a bad partner when you fall in love with someone new.

Our flock and the whole bird rescue project has been our boon, our safe harbor when the rest of our world didn't seem to understand. In the day-to-day, it's what keeps us both going. And it's why, despite us both being happily poly, we're still just the two of us and the birds.

"That's why I didn't tell Kai about my feelings for him."

"Because you had to home to make sure Koko was okay?"

"No, not that exactly. I just don't think he'd get it. How important everything is to me. You, Koko, the flock, the animal rescue, the pollinators dying all across the world -- all of it. It wasn't just an issue of about being non-binary and queer and poly, really. I just didn't think he was ready for all that stuff. We'd only just met."

"You say *all that* stuff like those are bad things about you," Maritza says with a frown.

"I just think it's hard for some people to understand."

Maritza shrugs but looks sad. And, I feel sad admitting she's right. I was worried *I'd* be a deal-breaker. So, I never brought it up.

"You're right. It wasn't fair to myself," I admit at length. "But it's too late. That was the choice I made."

Maritza rubs my hand in a way that says she understands. We both hide pieces of ourselves at times. Never from each other, and that's what keeps us together. We can be both be whole with each other. And we know we're fully loved.

I give Maritza's hand a squeeze back, holding her fingers tight against mine.

Silence fills the car for the rest of the drive home. It's not a tense silence, but a contemplative one. In it, I reflect over all the possible realities that might come to pass with me leaving O'ahu and coming back to the Pacific Northwest. I don't see any route that feels as big as working for the insect conversation project on the islands did, but that ship has sailed. I can close my eyes and reread the whole email. All the facts the department quoted were wrong, but it is what it is. A no.

Besides, I have Mariza and the flock to think about. Even if I didn't like the answer I got in regards to the job, it was time to come home.

Mariza pulls our little electric car into driveway and we get out in unison. I unravel the extension chord, pull out the batteries from the back of the car, and set them up to charge. Our car isn't one of those fancy new looks-like-a-car electric cars. Our's is a three-wheeled contraption dreamed up by a couple of very clever engineer friends we acquired from the same conservation camp where we met ten years ago. The little car is nothing much to look at, and it could use a new coat of paint, but it runs from point A to point B, and it carries luggage we can't fit on our bikes.

After setting the batteries up to charge, Mariza goes into the house ahead of me and starts riling up the flock with anticipation of my return. As soon as I open the door and call out, I get a whirlwind of ecstatic parrots of all shapes, sizes, and colors all making their unique flock calls. The sound is deafening and pleasant, and I'm caught up in a whirlwind of feathers and a rush of seed-scented air. Birds land on my arms, my shoulders, my head, cling to the back collar of my sweater.

"My truest of loves," I say tenderly.

We kiss one another like humans and birds kiss. I make kissy noises while a dozen little beaks nibble the tip of my nose, the corners of my eyes, the hair around my ear lobes. When they're satisfied, the birds chirp and all fly off together, fluttering back to the perches and play stations from whence they came.

I turn to Mariza, and my smile is so huge it feels ready to split my face in two.

"So few people truly understand how much love birds have to give."

Mariza tsks her tongue at me. "Yes, but sometimes, you sell people short, mi amor."

I know what she's talking about. Not birds, but Kai.

I let the comment hang, replying with a sad sigh and go looking for Koko. I find the little conure sitting on their favorite play station with one leg and one wing extended in a graceful stretch. We've never gotten Koko sexed due to health issues, and I'm happy enough to consider them my little non-binary bird advocate.

We eye each other and Koko leans forward eagerly. They haven't tried to fly to me because the craziness of the flock intimidates them when they're not feeling well. But now, they see me looking right at them, and they call out my name. I reach for them, and they stretch their beak toward me, wings flapping. I move closer so they don't have far to flap and hold my hand out.

"Come on, beautiful," I say gently. "You can do it."

Koko leans out over the perch, hesitates, then jumps and takes wing unevenly. They wobble toward me on a partially lame wing that we've been working on strengthening. They manage to land on my hand even if unevenly. They nuzzle my palm in victory, rubbing their soft head between my thumb and forefinger while chipping happily. Instantly, I can feel just how much weight they've lost in my absence. I give Mariza a worried frown.

"You took them in?"

"Tres veces. Three times. The vet said they need a specialist at this point. They've done all they can."

"But..." I reached for words. "Those were specialists."

"We need specialier specialists. There's a load of tests we need to run, but the vets at our office can't do any of them on smaller birds. Didn't you say something about a small bird specialist on Maui you heard about while you were there?"

"Yeah, but they don't allow birds to travel into the islands without shipping them. I'm not shipping Koko. Not in this state."

Mariza looks down and sighs, sounding as depressed as I feel. "What about your local boy? Does he know anyone? Connections are everything."

"First of all, he's not *my* local boy. And, honestly, I don't know. We never talked about ourselves, really. We mostly talked broad spectrum stuff. We made puns and laughed a lot. Our private lives never really came up."

"You don't think he'd be willing to help?"

"I don't know that he *could* help, is what I'm saying."

"But, you never asked."

"No."

"So, why not try? You seem to think he's gentle and kind."

"He is, without a doubt!" I defend. "He's one of the kindest people I've ever met."

My cheeks flush as I think of his gentle face, his sweet laugh, his bright smile that could warm a body chilled to the bone. I look up again and Mariza has that giddy look of excitement she gets when I'm daydreaming about someone else.

"Si? Tell me more!" Mariza says, graciously allowing us to divert a heavy subject for a better time. She nudges my side when I play coy, hesitating shyly. "Oh, come on. Spill the beans already!"

It's easy to gush to Mariza about Kai once I get started. The image of his strong yet gentle arms rise up around me like a careful embrace. I can smell his cologne again, rich and sweet. I can taste the sea on my lips and feel his long course black hair tickling my cheek. Overhead, ripe coconuts clatter together in time to the beats of my heart. Over our shoulders, the red sun disappears below the crystalline blue line of the ocean horizon. Caught in a sudden cool gust, white and yellow plumerias fall around our heads as we part ways, not frowning but not smiling either. A single pink plumeria lands in my hand and I pocket it for safe keeping.

It's a scene right out of a Harlequin romance, and I tell Mariza all about it. Our last beach walk, our last conversation, our last hug, and that terrible strained and silent goodbye.

I pull the flower from my pocket. It's crushed now, bruised and brown. I hand it to Mariza. "Not as pretty as the ones in photographs, but I tried to bring it back for you."

"Keep it. It's your memory, not mine."

I take the ruined flower, fold it gingerly, and press it between my palms. "Thank you," I say in a whisper. I can't decide if I'm talking to Mariza, to Kai, or to the plumeria tree for giving me this one last memory.

Mariza rubs my shoulder lovingly. "I can't wait to meet him."

"I don't think that'll ever happen. When exactly are we going to fly to Maui together? Who would take care of the birds? Think of Koko."

Mariza waves my excuses away, then she shifts gears. She puts on her serious face and clears her throat. When she gets down to business, she stops code switching into Spanish, and her face takes on a calculated edge.

She's had to hide her accent, her heritage, and just about anything Mexican about her from shitty co-workers and racist superiors at the very white university. The effects on her personality are clear, and it bothers me. I've tried to tell her she doesn't have to put on her "white scientist" face around me, but it's habit. It makes my heart ache because all I want in the world is to find a place for us where she doesn't have to hide her roots.

In a fantasy, that place had been Hawai'i. The both of us surrounded by locals who value other cultures far more than Westerners do right now. But, that was a wild dream and not reality.

This is reality, and I should be listening.

Maritza asks, "So, how many rare varieties of pollinators did you find thriving on the island?"

"Thriving? Zero. Still alive?" I think for a minute, quickly trying to corroborate data in my mind for a quick guesstimate. "Maybe three dozen."

"That's it?!" Mariza's shock is genuine. She's sad and shaken, and I love her for how much she cares.

I nod, my own chest tightening at the thought. Less butterfly varieties equals less population stability equals more extinctions when the next round of germicide improvements come out from the gears of industrial farm multinational corporations focused on making a buck, not keeping a planet and all its people alive.

"Any new evolution patterns?" Mariza asks hopeful.

"None that are observable," I say, then add a quiet, "yet."

It's ridiculous optimism that makes me say it. This hope that evolution can somehow outpace the rate of human destruction causing mass extinctions across the globe. The worst and first victims are the insect world, largely because humanity seems bent on seeing them as our enemies. So, people just don't care if they disappear from existence.

It's foolish and short-sighted. Insects make up a huge percentage of the Earth's biomass. Without them, there are no eco-systems left alive. Without them, there are no fruits or vegetables. Without them, we're all dead.

But humans have never liked what they don't understand.

Take for example: the caterpillar. Despite how highly praised and adored their beautiful wafting colorful winged counterparts are, a huge variety of caterpillars are on the high risk list. And what people don't seem to realize is that without this loathed counterpart, the butterfly is dead on arrival.

It's a systemic issue. One that big corporate farms and chemical companies have perpetuated through effective advertising. Dismantling a whole system is impossible in the amount of time we conservationists have left, but we also don't have any other plan.

It's a losing battle no matter how you look at it. We aren't big enough and we can't fight hard or fast enough. Some days, I feel like the world is Koko, and nothing I can do is enough.

The specialer specialists we need to fix things just don't exist.

"You did what you could do," Mariza tries to cheer me up. "What ever happened to the director of conservation affairs position you applied for at the research center? Did they ever get back to you?"

"Right before I left, yes. I got declined."

"No way. You're the most qualified person alive!"

"It wasn't the department's choice. It was lobbyists. The funding got pulled for conservation on O'ahu. There will be no department-specific directors. Just a single head running the program and an obscene number of volunteers."

"They can't actually expect to get any real work done like that."

"No, they don't. But without the funding, they've got no choice. It's run the program using volunteers or shut the facility down altogether."

"What if we started our own non-profit non-gov agency to supplement their programs? The government can't shut us down if we aren't asking them for money."

"That's a brilliant idea, only how? We aren't Hawai'ian. We don't even live there."

"No, but you know someone who is and who does."

"That again. I thought we were saving the Kai conversation for another time?" I complain.

"We are. I'm not asking you to ask him to marry us or something. I just think: you never know. He might be able to help us out."

"You just want to move to Hawai'i, don't you?" I tease, avoiding the difficult subject again.

"I just want us all to be happy," Mariza says all too knowingly.

"I am happy. Here. With the flock. And you."

"I know," Mariza kisses my forehead. "But you always want more, too."

She isn't wrong. She knows me all too well.

"I want more for you, yes. And Koko. But, I just don't see how."

"Talk to that local boy of your's, will you? For me?" Mariza urges.

I can hear all our birds in the background singing and chirping along, and it sounds like the ocean before a storm. And I see the thunderheads over my head that last moment on Maui with Kai's hand in mine.

And I can't say why, but something feels big and important about trying again.

"Okay, I'll send him an email tomorrow. But, he's not mine."

"Not yet," Maritza winks at me. "Now, come into our room and let's relax."

Mariza leads me into our bedroom by the hand. I know she's been planning this night since I left. I across the threshold and smell rare flowers and endangered herbs that only grow in the hot houses she works tirelessly in. I'm enveloped in the air of mountain meadows that no longer exist and a colder, sharper sea air tinged with seaweeds and kelp on the verge of extinction.

Mariza wraps her soft but strong arms around my middle, and I feel like a ship coming into harbor before a terrible storm. Her eyes are lighthouses and I'm guided into her body like a boat needing anchor.

The waves of love rise all around us, smelling of human sweet and salt.

Maritza kisses my neck, runs her hands along my thighs, nuzzles her soft nose into my shoulder, lips nibbling my collar bone. And in a hot, raging wave of passion, everything else is swept away. There is no Koko. No Kai. No here nor there, no Hawai'i, Pacific Northwest, insect biomass or rare plants.

There is only this room, Maritza, and our love burning so bright.

I fall into her rhythm so easily, smooth and steady and sweet.

And yet, in between the beats of our hearts, there flows something new. Deep below us, an undertow begins to pull, heavy and strong. It tugs at my core, pulling me away from this moment on to something more.

It's a current drawing the ship of us out to sea; tossing, complicated, but more beautiful than anything I've ever seen.

I'm both excited and terrified.

# Kailua

I don't call Kai in the morning because I'm too scared, but I do send him an email.

I take my laptop off the kitchen table after feeding the birds, sit in my regular work-chair, and set it. Maritza wakes up later than me, spends time with Koko, and then meanders over and offers me a hot coffee. I breathe in the aromatic smell of roasted caramel, salted chocolate, and vanilla beans. The smell alone is soothing. I take a sip and set in.

In the email, I tell Kai in brief detail about my life. I talk about Mariza and her plants, myself and my insect research. I talk at length about Koko and the flock and our work with rescuing birds. I dig down deeper into Koko's plight, which is easy for me to do. I mention very briefly the specialists here who've fallen short, mentioning the specialer specialists on Maui who might not. I ask if Kai knows anything at all about bird transport to the islands from the mainland. I don't get specific. I leave it at that. I sign off with "All the best."

I show the email to Maritza before I hit send.

She comes over, still in her robe. She kisses the top of my head, takes my laptop in her hands, and sits on my lap. When she's done, she looks down at me with a frown.

"What?"

"This sounds like an introduction to a letter to a potential donor for a project you hope to get off the ground in a year or so," she says.

"What do you mean?" I ask, trying to keep the offense out of my voice. I fail and Maritza stands, handing the computer back into my hands.

"Distant. Impersonal."

*Don't say it.*

"Muy frio. So cold."

I roll my eyes, frustrated. I'm about to argue, but I know better. I re-read the email. "Okay. I see what you mean. But...how would you phrase it?"

"Honestly."

"Easy for you to say," I huff and re-situate the laptop back into my lap. "You don't have a crush on him."

Maritza winks at me and nods.

After four hours, I have a draft of reasonable length and considerable warmth. Maritza reads it and gives my shoulder a squeeze.

"That's the Jun I know and love."

I hit send. And in a matter of minutes, I have a reply from Kai.

The email is surprisingly short.

[I think I have a way to get Koko to that specialist. Do you trust me?]

That's it. I show the email to Maritza.

"Vos si? Do you?" she asks.

"I do."

"Contestale. Answer him."

I hesitate.

"No? You don't then," Maritza challenges.

"I do, but--"

"Pero que?"

"I'm worried about the flock, you, us."

"Don't be," Maritza says with a sharp snap that makes me worry more, not less.

I start typing, and the result is not what I expected. I meant to write up a simple description of Koko's issues. Instead, what I craft is a lengthy, heady explanation of the ideologies of polyamory, the importance of the transparency, and my place in the scope of my core nesting relationship. I make a lot of allusions to birds. I mention Koko and draw connections between Koko and Maritza, between my family and my place in the world. Then, at the end, I type something I never meant to type.

[I love you.]

Maritza squeezes my shoulder in that way -- firm and warm -- that says, "Buen."

That feeling from last night -- that heavy pull -- drags on my gut. And I know that I should just hit send without second-guessing myself. But, can I really say all of this? To Kai, who didn't ask for all this TMI about my life? Who simply said, "I think I can help your sick bird." Am I reading too much into this?

The heavy feeling in my gut grows stronger, and I can almost feel Kai's hand in mine. We're standing on the beach, the sea-touched wind in our hair, and I can taste his smell on my lips. On my other side, there's Maritza and her hand is so warm, so soft in mine. Across the wide open horizon, a dark storm cloud approaches -- but I'm not afraid.

The vision is gone as quickly as it came on. I shake my head and look at my screen to see that my hand has already hit [send].

"Well, that's that," I say and stand.

Marizta plants a kiss on my cheek. "Si. You did the right thing."

"I don't know about that."

I'm so uncertain that I check my phone for an email update every few seconds. In a matter of minutes, I have see Kai's reply in my inbox. I open it on my phone immediately.

[Jun, I want to help your ohana come to Maui. Will you let me?]

I show the screen to Maritza, my heart hammering.

"What does he mean? What do I say? What the what?"

"It sounds to me like he knows a way we can get the birds to Maui."

"But that's impossible. It can't be done."

"I think your local boy is telling you that it can be."

"Fine, maybe he knows an airline pilot or something. But....what about the rest of it?"

Maritza points at the screen and shrugs. "No se. He didn't say."

"That's scary," I say.

My skin tightens and chills slither across my whole body. I think of all the people I've met -- kind, amazing people -- who couldn't handle my polyamory. I feel all the scars where my heart broke over loves lost because they didn't understand Maritza and me. Or they didn't understand the birds. Or, they didn't understand my work with the insects. Or, they couldn't wrap their head around the importance of all three in my life.

It's never their fault. But trying again when you know what you're up against -- it gets harder every time. And Kai is someone I don't want to think of in the shape of scars left on my heart. I'd rather keep what we had in my treasury. The sweetness, the companionable company, the peace. I don't want to ruin it all by taking a foolish chance.

"If it were me," Maritza breaks into my thoughts, "I'd say si."

I chew on that while I spend the rest of the day with Koko.

Around evening, my cell phone rings. I glance at the number and it's a number I don't recognize. My caller ID says the caller's name is Ohana Shipping Co and the area code is (808). It's coming from a shipping company in Hawai'i?

My gut drops. My skin tightens. Didn't I explain Koko's situation well enough? I feel sick to my stomach as I pick the phone up.

"Hello?"

"Jun?" Kai's sweet voice greets my ear.

"What?" I blurt out, shocked.

"Sorry, I'm calling from my work number. But, I wanted to get the ball rolling as soon as we could. I need to work out my schedule well in advance to ensure that I'm the one on the ground to load Koko in and unload them in Maui. I figured, let's not waste any time. What do you say?"

Kai works for a shipping company. And that shipping company handles animals. No, correction. Kai is going to personally ensure Koko is taken care of. What's more, he'll be on the plane the whole way.

How can this be? It's too perfect. Perfect doesn't happen to me or Koko. I'm stunned into silence, and Kai's question hangs between us on the line.

"Jun?"

"I...uh...yeah...I'm sorry. I just had no idea you...how is this even possible?"

"Must be meant to be," Kai says gently and his laugh is so sweet. It's the sound of gentle waves washing a long sandy shore. I can almost feel my toes, warm in the sand, drenched in the sudden rush of cool refreshing water. I can hear the palm trees. I can see the orange glow of the evening sun touching the distant watery horizon. That pull in my gut gets stronger, undeniable.

But, as a scientist, I don't believe in fate, magical connections, or "everything happens for a reason." I believe in evidence and proof. Coincidences can be wild and opportunistic, but they're just coincidences. Right?

Maritza comes over from her study table, takes one look at my blanched face and reaches for the phone.

"Let me talk?"

I hand the phone over without resistance because I'm at a loss for words. The universe just handed me exactly what I wanted, and instead, my heart is hammering in my throat and I feel a little nauseous. I need to process this alone.

Well, not exactly.

I need to process this with my birds.

I leave Maritza on the phone with Kai and head toward the bird room to wrestle with this tug-of-war between my gut and my intellect. I open the door to find the whole flock happily preening, getting themselves ready for sleep. I find Koko on the lowest perch in one of the large flight cages. Koko's sitting on a large branch Maritza gathered from a dead koa tree in the field one day. Koko loves to sit on it because it's easy to get to but still high enough off the ground to feel safe.

As soon as I come close, Koko perks up and climbs aboard my shoulder. I offer them treats while I whistle a tune to myself. Koko rejects the snacks and instead nuzzles deep against my neck and joins me in singing softly. I rub Koko's head while I think. I don't always understand Koko's motivation. So often, they reject the rewards I offer them for stepping up, perching on my arm, or climbing onto my shoulder, as if they'd rather let me know they're choosing to do so because they want to. As if just choosing to be together is enough.

It's enough for me, but I wouldn't expect it to be enough for Koko. Or Maritza.

Or...Kai.

I shake my head, rattling free the errant thought.

Just because Kai works for a shipping company and is agreeing to help Maritza and I get Koko to the specialists on Maui does *not* mean we are going to be together. It doesn't mean he's interested in me romantically. It doesn't mean anything more than he is a very kind, very generous person who wants to help a hurting bird.

I rub the top of Koko's head as they preen the side of my hair.

After about twenty minutes, Koko decides they've had enough people time, and they squawk loudly and hops off my shoulder to climb back to their perch, leaving my ear ringing and my shoulder feeling empty. I sigh, get up, and go back into the other room to collect my phone.

I come back into the living room to find Maritza splayed out on the couch, phone in hand, chatting and laughing happily. At first, I think someone else must have called. A friend from the Queer POC Alliance or someone from our bi-weekly queer poly meet up? A Seattlite for sure. Someone to miss.

But, no. The closer I get, the more I can hear. And while Maritza is still talking in her natural lightly accented English, something's off. The conversation is all about native Hawai'ian plants. A topic none of our friends would know anything about. Except for...

"Are you still talking to Kai?" I ask, stunned.

Maritza looks up at me with a glitter in her eyes. "He knows so much. He used to be a taro farmer, you know?"

*I didn't know,* I almost say and feel a tinge of jealousy. But then, the warning signal fades and I correct myself, shocked to find the truth buried somewhere in my memory.

"I did, actually. He mentioned it once, in passing, over coffee. I don't know why it never occurred to me to mention it to you. I'm sorry."

"Don't be," Maritza says with grace, "he says he hardly remembers mentioning it himself."

It's true. We were always so wrapped up in philosophy and talking about the bigger picture.

I hear Maritza's honey-tinged laughter. A full-belly rumbling joy bubbles up from her throat and coats my ears in sweet oil. My socialized logic ought to tell me to be jealous that Kai and Maritza are still talking, hitting it off so well. And, shouldn't I be worried that they'll become better friends than Kai and me. I should be angry.

But, that's not how I feel at all. Instead, my heart swells with joy at their excitement for each other. Compersion, I think with a smile, is like the happy optimistic twin to jealousy. I watch Maritza's somber eyes light up and a smile spread like oil across her face. It's an expression she makes when I surprise her with little things, and I love seeing it on her face.

A mix of guilt and excitement flutter around in my chest like a struggling bird trying to fly. I know I should deny it, but I can't. I really like the thought that Kai makes her happy like that. My skin prickles without my permission at a sudden irrational vision of a living room with the birds flying free, Koko on my shoulder, Kai's hand in Maritza's, and my head on her shoulder. We're eating dinner together discussing the challenges and dangers facing native plants and insects as international import of invasive species increases with decreasing governmental power and little corporate regulations taking over. We all have something to add. Koko and the other birds happily chirp and sing along to the commotion, alighting on our shoulders as they choose. In this irrational dream, Koko chooses me time and time again.

Those green feathers and those little clawed feet are like a blessing from the air, willing me to dream. But, instead, I shake the vision away. I turn my eyes back to Maritza, who blushes deeply as soon as her eyes meet mine. Again, I'm flooded with warmth.

Just maybe, one day, the three of us could give it a try.

*Not right now. The timing's all wrong,* I chide myself silently.

"You want to talk to Jun about it?" Maritza says into the phone, pauses, and hands my cell phone back to me. She winks and goes to the room where Koko is playfully screaming at the top of their lungs.

"It's me," I say, suddenly uncertain, shyer than I've felt in a long time.

"Maritza says you're worried, and I understand that. I do."

Kai's slipped into his own natural Hawai'ian accent. My heart warms at the sound. We are all three from different cultures, but we share common ground. Being Hawai'ian or half-Japanese or half-Mexican in modern America puts us all in the same situation of living in a soceity that doesn't want to see or acknowledge us. Like Maritza hiding her accent, I hide behind a passing whiteness that few rarely question. Kai, on the other hand, stands out like a beautiful ominous cloud on the horizon. Dark, bold and unavoidable.

I long for more of that strength in my life. I wonder silently if Maritza does too.

"Jun, are you listening?" Kai brings me back to the conversation.

"Not exactly," I admit. "I'm sorry. What were you saying?"

"I was saying that Maritza and I agree. We have to think about Koko first. Don't you agree?"

I catch on Kai's words, and my heart leaps into my throat.

*We.*

Like the three of us are something. An item. And, dare I think? An ohana, as Kai would say. A family who takes care of one another no matter what.

I feel something bloom and open up inside of me. A feeling of belonging, of things being as they should be. And I know it's irrational, but I feel like I've found something I'd been waiting my whole married life to find: someone who fills a slot in our lives we didn't even know we had. A missing piece we hadn't even realized we lacked. Until here he is, right in front of us saying *we* and *us* like it's the most natural thing in the world.

I shake my head. It can't be that easy. Nothing is that easy.

"Jun?" Kai asks.

I sigh. "You're right. Of course, you're right. I'm just...I can't believe I didn't know you worked in air shipping. That's...well, it's just too coincidental. It's almost..."

"Made to be?" Kai says with a playful slant.

"Yes, but I don't personally believe in that."

"What's not to believe?" Kai challenges me softly just like he did on the beach before I left Hawai'i.

I catch on his words this time before he explains himself.

What *is* there not to believe? The facts are right in front of me.

Koko needs to be shipped to Maui. I went to Hawai'i looking for something I needed, and I found Kai. Just because we never talked about our jobs doesn't mean we didn't share our full selves. Obviously, Kai understood without my saying how important my birds and my relationship with Maritza is. And it's not like I couldn't guess what is important to Kai, if I genuinely tried.

I never tried because I was afraid of what the truth meant.

That I'd found someone willing to love me for me, accepting that my partner Martiza and my bird family would always be two pieces of my whole. I was scared that, in Kai, I'd found what I needed but hadn't been looking for.

A blessing from the sky at just the right time.

Not coincidence, but an intuitive drive toward a goal we both wanted. A decision made intentionally, if subconsciously, by both of us.

"You're right," I say at length. "We made it happen. That I believe in."

"Good. Then, you'll come to Maui?"

"Is it possible? I mean, isn't there a lot of paperwork and red tape to bring a bird in and out of Hawai'i? Particularly, a bird that's less than one-hundred percent? I just don't know if we should put Koko through all that."

"I agree. If you come, you should stay."

I look up at Maritza, shocked at what Kai's implying.

Maritza gives me a thumbs up.

"But--" I start.

Kai chuckles. "Mari said you'd argue. But you know, there's a some good conservation jobs on Maui."

"What?!"

"Mari told me what you two do. And we talked about the research institutes on Maui. I have an Uncle who works in the building as a receptionist and an Auntie in the field. There's no reason we couldn't find something for you two. Maui desperately needs people, unlike O'ahu. And..."

Kai's voice hangs in the air.

"And?" I echo.

My cheeks go flush. He isn't about to say what I think he's going to say. He just isn't.

"I'd get to see more of you."

I blink. "I'm not exactly single," I say to be clear.

"I know. Mari explained."

"And you're *okay* with that?"

"What's not to be okay with?" Kai says in true Kai fashion.

"I...nothing but...I just thought...you wouldn't believe in that sort of thing.

"What's not to believe in?"

I laugh out loud. Maritza comes over and rubs my shoulder in a familiar way that says "I hope what I did was okay." She means telling Kai more than I ever did. She means blowing my cover.

I smile and nod at her, my hand touching her's gently.

Yes, it's okay. I'm scared, sure, but not angry. Kai deserves the truth, and I wanted him to know it. I just couldn't have found the words. But Maritza could, and that's what I love about her so much. She knows how to be strong when I can't see a way through. It's her mother in her. An unbelievably strong Mexican woman who crossed the desert alone to get to California in order to give her soon-to-be-born daughter an opportunity at a life she never had.

Maritza is her mother through and through, forging on when the world tells her to back down and shut up. She's my strength and I couldn't say what I'm about to say without her by my side.

"Okay, we'll come."

"Good. I'll get to work. Call you soon."

Kai and I say goodbye as butterflies gather in my stomach. I toss the phone once Kai hangs up, and I sink into Maritza's body like the listless boat I am coming back into harbor. The storm may rage on overhead, but I know that here, I'm safe and sound.

"I can't believe we just had that conversation," I mumble into Maritza's chest.

She strokes my head gingerly.

"What's there not to believe?" she asks in a voice that almost sounds like Kai's.

I laugh, pulling her closer to me and breathing in her skin and hair.

In a rush of realization, I understand why I was so worried about placing the name of the flowers Kai gave me. It's because Maritza smells just like fresh plumerias. Every strand of her hair is a good memory, every drop of sweat is a blessing from the world.

I can't wait to see Kai in his shipping gear. I can't wait to see the three of us altogether. I can't wait to see Koko, healed and healthy, finally able to take wing and fly. I know whatever happens next is going to be one wild storm. And yet, I can't wait to be drenched in an oncoming rain, water pouring down the sides of my body, soaking me in a million plumeria-scented blessings from the sky.

* * *

# COME SUMMER, COME WINTER, *I'll Come for You*

"A breathtakingly beautiful story. One of my favorites."
-Kristine Kathryn Rusch
*New York Times* Bestselling Author

## REI ROSENQUIST

CHAPTER 1

*Summer*

*T*okyo, 2014

Through low grey-brown smoggy-looking clouds, the morning sun peaks through. The color, a shockingly dull and far away yellow-orange. The heat is already heavy, damp, absolutely suffocating. A waterlogged wool blanket that scratches at throats, stuffs up lungs, and makes the whole city collectively cough and choke.

As I descend the rickety metal stairs of my ugly industrial cookie-cutter apartment complex, the back of my neck is already wet. Rushing to cross the street before the blinking green light turns to red, my thighs slip slickly past one another. So much for the fresh nylons I unpacked mere minutes ago.

The package promised to help with this kind of thing – airing out summer sweat that trickles down your inner thighs like dirty rivers headed to the sea of gross pooling in the bottom of each shoe. A waste of 100 yen.

But then, it *was* in Japanese, so maybe I misread a kanji. Or all of them.

My bad.

I keep on down the sidewalk, sticking to the right side of the raised yellow stripe, dragging myself along at a pathetic pace. Staring down the road toward my destination, I sigh wearily.

Harajuku Station.

It's so far away and I'm already tired. Long Tokyo hours of bland web design work will do that.

I blink a few times, trying to see through the thick haze all around me. No use. Humidity clings to my eyelashes and eyebrows. It covers the city in a not-quite-sheer film of misery. If only I could find something exciting. Today is a shot at that. A better life.

A drop of sweat trickles from my hairline, a slow snake slipping across my forehead, and drips into my eye. I wipe it away with the small square towel with cutesy trees that smile at me. I keep forgetting to change it out. I don't know what's wrong with me. It smells of mildew. Just like the rest of my clothes, my closet, my apartment, all of Tokyo.

One more reason to hate Tokyo's summertime. "Tsuyuu" they call it, which can mean either "plum season" or "season of mildew and mold" depending on which kanji is used.

Unlike loads of other kanji, I understand the reason for this variation perfectly.

I stuff the nasty towel back in the front pocket of my over-sized fake leather handbag as I arrive at the front of the station. Finally. I peep in with my green penguin pass card, climb the stairs, and huff as I see my fate laid out before me.

The clock overhead reads five o'clock pm, dead.

Rush hour.

And, like a typical Monday, the place is jam-packed. Sweaty bodies wall to wall on the platform, crammed against one another's moldy raincoats and damp suit jackets. The train's headlamp strikes the platform through the mist, diffuse and powder pale.

But I, unlike the masses, am not headed home from work. I'm headed out from my home office for a date.

As if cued by the light, the rain starts. A rushing gush like a faucet's been turned on. The train hisses into the station. Wheels whine and scream like angry children as the conductor hits the brakes. Metal wheels grind against the suddenly wet tracks, stuttering to a halt.

I sag. Inside the train, window to window, it's more bodies. Last in line, I pack myself in by grabbing the roof of the train with my fingers and pressing my back against an elderly man and a couple of young kids in school uniforms. Nobody can move.

The doors close across my nose, and I feel like a dead fish in a sealed can. I release myself to the pressure of bodies pressing against me. Conditioned air blows from the maxed out "airkon" overhead, but by the time it hits me, it's already rank with the tang of sweat. It wraps me in the top of my head and fills my mouth with stale air. The taste of Tokyo in the summertime.

The train lurches into forward and the bodies all sway as one. For the next five minutes, we are all stuck in whatever position we chose. Accidental or not. I distract myself by watching outside as drenched strangers duck under ruined umbrellas turned wholly inside out. Someone discards one with a black handle and clear plastic top into the gutter where it clatters down to join the graveyard of many an umbrella who's shared its fate. Broken by Tokyo's relentless summer.

I feel that umbrella's pain.

Everything is soaked from head to toe, down to my underpants. My bag is dripping from the bottom, pitter-patting against my bare ankles. Low pumps and a skirt. What was I thinking? Poor choice for typhoon season. But then, in the torrential downpours of Tokyo's mid-summer, everything feels like a mistake.

Don't even try. Just throw the drenched mildew-ridden towel in.

Finally, the train pulls into my destination: Shibuya station.

My spirits rise thinking of my sole reason for braving the weather today. Meeting someone genuinely interesting from that wretched dating site my friend dared me to join. I try not to get my hopes up high. A short fling would be nice. Momentary end of isolation. Something new and exciting to mix up the daily hum-drum of web design. That'd be a good change.

I disembark and push through the crush, looking out for the yellow 出口 sign that reads "Hachiko" in big fat Roman letters. It's the most stereotypical place in all of the 23 wards we could have met, but when you said you wanted to meet, I'd have jumped for anything.

I come up the long set of dripping stairs and out into the open air. The typhoon is still dumping its worst and there's water everywhere. Hachiko plaza has become a pond. Nobody is there, aside from you.

I instantly recognize you from the picture you texted me. Small and slight, dressed in a long black coat, dark grey and cream lace decorating the hem and sleeves. Knee high chunky lace-up black boots. A big floppy black hat dripping in more lace covers your face, a strip of pewter colored chiffon shrouds you in mystery from me.

Very early 1990's goth. Adorable.

You look my way and wave a gloved hand. Then, you do something crazy. Rip off your hat, crumple it in your hand, and dash toward me. By the time you are at my side, you are drenched from head to toe. Just like me. I bet your underwear are soaked, too.

*Not like that,* I chide myself and step out, umbrella-less into the day.

You rush up so quick I can't look at your face. Your hand slips effortlessly into mine. A soft round nose nuzzles against my neck and your high, light voice purrs above the roar of the rain.

"Let's go have fun, love!" in a shockingly un-Japanese way and I find myself doubting that you are a native born Tokyo resident.

My blood boils. My stomach goes cold. "O-okay," I stammer helplessly.

You pull me along. By the time we duck out of the rain, we look like two swimmers who've finished a triathlon but forgot to change their clothes. Everything clings. Might as well be naked, I think and turn red hot. I try not to stare. You smile like you know my struggle and slide open the narrow glass door to a restaurant who's name I can't see for all the rain and haze.

A tuxedoed maitre de comes rushing up, speaking in high polite Japanese. You don't hesitate to take the lead and ramble back something I have no hope of understanding, which reaffirms your citizenship. Japanese without a question mark.

The maitre de bows low at the waist and lead us to seats. White table cloth. Rose in a crystal vase. Multiple forks of multiple sizes for multiple purposes. I stare not at the table of this ritzy ordeal, but at you.

Your eyes are watch catch me. Black opals steal the light of the room and swallow it, spitting back only mysterious unknown. Your face is softly round, your cheeks high, your lips a thin red painted line. Mascara exaggerates the upward swoosh of your long, luxurious eyelashes. I could get lost in there, a mysterious forest of black bamboo.

I open my mouth to attempt something clever, but all I can think of is the weather. Then, I recall we've been calling each other by Line user names.

"I'm Sammy," I say. "It's nice to finally meet you…"

"Mikata," you grin devilishly. "And you are far more beautiful than your profile pics."

My blush deepens and all the discomfort of the typhoon melts away.

You reach a thin delicate hand across the table and take up mine, made of callouses and big bones. You squeeze my palm with impressive strength. "I like you. Let's stick together."

"Okay," I reply without hesitation.

You smile in a way that says my answer means something big.

"I like you, too," I say partly to fill the awkward silence I can feel coming on and partly, I realize, because I mean it. You are something rare, and I don't want to let go.

We polish off our meal and bottle of wine in what feels like the passing of a thought.

My heart sinks when you stand. "Time to go?"

You head shakes, locks of silky black hair dancing about. "No. Tonight is Hanabi."

My eyes light up at the mention of Tokyo's famous summer fireworks show. "I've never seen it."

"I know a place we can get in. Let's go."

I jump up excitedly. "Okay."

Outside, the sky has cleared, but the sun is already slipping below the horizon. The light is turning blue-grey. Post-storm humidity hangs on the horizon, a thin film of the golden light stretching across all of central Tokyo like a dome. We walk the city hand in hand while that band of color in the sky turns from gold to orange. The blue dome of the sky deepens toward black, and the handful of city-visible stars come out.

"The fireworks start soon," you say and duck into a subway station.

I follow blindly, led by the arm. We come out at Kite-sando and head up the crowded street.

Across the city, rooftop pop up restaurants are jammed wall to temporary wall with people waiting. All of them are standing room only. For the early comers, there are tables spread with white table cloths and glasses for wine. As the evening wears on, waiters dressed in long dress-like aprons bring small dishes of a variety of meats, grilled vegetables. For late comers, there is hours wait and maybe standing room only.

We didn't come early by any means, yet here we stand inside a ruby red velveteen rope. Along the far edge of the building where the rope ends, people shifting against one another's backs. We lean our bare arms lazily against the concrete ledge of the roof facing the direction the fireworks will come from. Optimal view, this. From the distant fans, a low breeze sweeps across the roof and attempts to dry our sweaty legs. It catches the edges of both of our short skirts and sends them swaying.

The smell of food is in the air, savory and sweet. A tray of mini pizzas swings by held high by a waiter dripping in sweat. I feel bad for the staff in this sweltering head. You cock your head at me and beckon the waiter over. I grab two pizzas and pass you one. The waiter wafts off like a melting ghost.

We prop half-full glasses of wine against each other's arms like we've been together for years. You sip your's just as the first red burst of light fills the sky. Then blue and white. Then, sparkles like a hundred stars. The lights dance across your face lightly, and I see you are frowning instead of smiling.

"What's the matter?"

"I want to tell you something."

"Go ahead," I sip my wine as purple light pops to life and dies out in a stuttering snap of silver and gold.

"I want to protect you, Sammy."

"No need," I say, feeling completely safe beside you on this rooftop.

You darken, leaning against me. "It's a family thing."

"Hm?" I say, distracted by the fireworks and the warmth of the wine.

"We're protectors," you say in a sly way I pretend not to notice. "Some people think we're gangsters, but in reality—"

"Gangsters? Like what, yakuza?" " I joke lightly, popping pepperoni into my mouth.

Your mouth opens but what comes out is swallowed by one of those big loud whizzy screaming hanabi go off. I don't bother to bring the question up again. It was just a joke and I'm having too much fun. You lean your head against my shoulder instead of my chest because we are the same height. I chuckle at how can't feel not thundering heartbeat, but rather the unshaken structure of my bones. Like I'm holding your head up.

"I'll always come for you," you say, life your head, and snog my face before I can say anything. And right then, the massive booming finale beings. We get lost in it, in each other, in the night and the tacky summer heat.

Everything is bliss.

# CHAPTER 2

# Winter

O*taru, 2016*

On every surface, snow is piled at least a meter thick. The air is aflutter with big chunky snowflakes. A wind howls and blows snow from nowhere to collect on the already heavy laden branches, walls, ledges of buildings and tops of roofs.

Overnight, the small huddled town of Otaru has been fully converted. The gentle powered sugar dusting has become an impenetrable tower of solid ice. Blocks of snow build up mountains out of shrubs, steps, and curbs. The landscape outside the window is treacherous, yes, but beautiful. Washed clean.

Maybe the snow could wash me too. Clear out the clutter of my heart. Clear the past. Make magic happen and let me find you today.

I open the hostel door, take a tentative step out into the entrance way, and am instantly covered in a downy snow. Clumps of snowflakes flutter by my nose, stick to my clothes, and get caught like dewdrops in the exposed locks of my hair.

I come back in, slide the ancient wooden door shut, and stand in the semi-warmth of the entrance way thinking of how warm we were two year ago in Tokyo during the hottest, wettest, stickiest summer on record.

"I want to protect you, Sammy," you'd said.

And stupid me, threw that away.

I don't even know why I ghosted you. It was so good, the weeks we spent together in your fancy high rise apartment. Too good. I panicked. And the slow fade out was all I could think to do to get away.

A blustery gust of wind carries flurries of snow across my face and over my shoulders. I tuck in deeper to my fluffy polyester scarf, knowing full well that as I nestle my nose deep in its warmth, the aging material is abrading into my lungs.

Things I try not to think too much about.

Like how childish I was at the end of that summer.

I should have called you. I could have messaged at least. Explained. Things were moving too fast. My job sucked. I had no money. I wanted to go back home to Hawaii. I didn't see how we could last.

But I didn't know how to say any of that, so I said nothing.

Then, right before summer ended, you messaged me. Said you were going north to escape the heat. You, honest and blunt, told me the truth. This was a test. To see if I loved you or if I had no guts.

You gave me all the details. The day you flew out and how Otaru was the last stop on the only train line that heads from New Chitose Airport. The address of the single hostel in all of the tiny port town would not have been hard to find. The name of your favorite cafe.

I should have gone. Met you at the train station in Otaru when you arrived. I should have taken the information, bought a ticket, and been there waiting.

I should have saved us.

But, I didn't. Out of some selfish desire to protect myself. At the time, it was less aware than that. I simply didn't respond, bought a different ticket, and shipped off to Hawaii, tail between my legs. Not running but mildly stepping away from the ledge you offered to jump off with me, hand in hand.

Truth? I was scared to death that if I jumped, I'd get swallowed up to my heart and head in love. The real deal, burning bright, the hottest on record in my life.

And then, I sat on the beach in Hawaii for two years and the mistake ate me alive.

So, I'm back now. In Otaru, not Tokyo. And it's winter, not summer.

But I'm trying to do things right. To find you and fix things. Like I should have.

Leaning my forehead against the window pane of the entrance way, staring out at the fluttering snow, I find resolve in this little pep talk to myself.

I puff up my chest, shove my hands in my pockets, and slide open the door again. It sticks half-way open and a bluster of snowy wind slaps me in the face. I crystallize against it. I have to get to the Owl Cafe. It's lunch time and if what you said two years ago is still right, you will be there.

It's worth a shot.

I step out. The chill wind sneaks its fingers under the edge of my coat and tickles my waist. Ahead of me, caught in updrafts from a vent, snow tussles about and drifts back lazily to the ground.

My feet make soft crunching sounds as I trudge across the street and down a series of stone steps that have become a steep slope indented hundreds of times with the hammers of boots and dogs' feet.

Up ahead, the red glowing paper lantern of where I'm headed. Painted in wide black brush stokes is the shop's name in kanji.

I can't read it.

If the shop's name were something easy to memorize like 田 (ta) or 山 (yama), I'd stand a chance. But "owl" is a complicated series of harried strokes my eyes can't make heads or tails of. "Cafe" is done in katakana, and I should be able to read that, but sometimes Katakana is harder to remember than kanji. So, no hope here.

If asked, I'd have to describe the big paper lantern instead. The doorway made of uneven sanded down logs, and the rope-wrapped glass orbs lined up. The wrinkled and peeling laminated paper menu tacked up to the wall of rough logs.

Outside, the cafe has a hodgy-podgy look. It seems popular here in the rustic down-to-earth port town. Whether it's a lack of resources or indigenous influence that creates the differences, I haven't figured out. But from what I see in photographs, al the buildings around Hokkaido are mottled, press board and clay, pasteboard and exposed screws. Logs, some sanded and some with the bark on, make up the majority of small mundane things. Door handles and toilet paper holders.

Owl Cafe is no exception.

I put my hand on a pale knotty sanded log and push open the waxed pasteboard door. In the entrance way, there are blue glass orbs of a variety of sizes balanced on trunks of the same pale wood, more set about at random on the floor, and still more hanging from dusty ropes overhead. I slide open the inner door of glass and blackened wood.

Inside is a cozy room with six well-used wooden tables and chairs of various shapes and sizes. Some are rusty metal, some wooden with crushed velvet cushions. One is subtly curved with a low rising back that curves ergonomically. A perfect fit. I head for it and the small square table it sits in front of.

At a long rugged but lovingly-used bar, the owner stands dressed in long sleeves and puffy down vest, face hidden behind a white mask. The owner eyes me, then dawdles. Shifting containers of coffee beans, wiping off the bar, arranging a stack of papers. Finally, with nothing left to do, the owner pads over and sets a glass of water before me.

"Ira shai ma se," a high polite voice sings out from behind a white medical mask.

"Arigato go zaimasu," I say in a spot-on accent.

The look of relief is immediate and the shop owner launches into the usual spiel of daily "o su su me" specials and what coffee is currently roasting. I already smell the hints of the Columbian beans caramelizing. It is less the scent of coffee and more like bread toasting. I nod happily, breathing it in and taking the cardboard menu written in ink pens and covered in cartoon stickers. I open it and feel an inward glow as the words come easily to me.

I'm just about to call out to have my order taken when the door chime goes off.

Someone steps in loudly, letting in a flurry of snow with them. I feel a rush of embarrassment for the outsider who's made a silly but rude mistake. I turn to look out of curiosity and my belly fills with butterflies.

"Sammy?" you gasp breathlessly, closing a black and cream lace-covered umbrella speckled of melting snowflakes. Still early 1990's goth. Amazing.

"Mikata," I gasp back. I'm caught between relief, excitement at the unexpected realization of my dream, and embarrassment that I've just associated you with an outsider who can't figure out how to close a Japanese door.

You rush over to my table, clonking across the floor in the same old chunky high heel boots. I'd have thought you'd break an ankle on these icy streets. Apparently not.

"What are you doing in Otaru?" you pull up a velvet cushioned chair and sit without the hesitation I'd feel in your position. Old ghost of a lover turning up out of nowhere appearing to read a menu in your indecipherable native tongue.

I can't bring myself to say the truth, so I come up with a lame excuse. "Vacation."

"Ha, me too."

"What?" I ask, confused.

"What what?" you prod. Never one for manners, you were.

"I-I don't know. I'd gotten the impression you lived here now."

"No, silly. I still live in the insufferable mess of Tokyo. But lucky you. I'm here for a week or two. My brother is getting married. Finally."

"Makoto? Isn't he younger than you?" I ask, challenging that 'finally' at the end of the sentence there. A very traditional concept for you. I find that strange.

"Yes, but he's big bother."

I don't really know what that means, but it sounds sexist. I cringe openly to make a point. "Shouldn't you be married too, then?"

You grin bigger than I thought you could. "Yes, in fact, I do. Thanks for asking."

"No, I—" I jump up, knocking over the small low backed chair.

From the bar, the owner looks up, concerned.

"Ah, sumimasen," I blunder. "Gomen'nasai. Ano..."

You laugh lightly, waving a hand in my direction. "Sumimasen. Kyo, kanojo to atta no wa hisashi buri no de hontoni bikurisugimashite, gomennasai."

"Iie iie," the shop owner says with a laugh, meaning "oh it's alright" basically.

The two of you ramble in Japanese too fluent and too quick for my ears to pick up. So, I sit back and think. What in hell am I going to do now? Ask if we can spend the day together? Confess my feelings and get that rip-the-bandage-off feeling over with? Say nothing and just see where things go?

I rule that last one out. I've spent enough time in my life drifting. That's how I lost you the first time. Given this outlandish second chance, that's about the last thing in the known universe I'm going to do.

What then?

"So," you turn back to me in perfect English. "I was thinking we could have a snack and then go for a stroll? I'd love to catch up."

"I was going to ask you the same thing."

You laugh and swat at my hand. "No, you weren't Sammy. You never do things like that."

"I was, actually," I say seriously and begin planning how to tell you the whole truth in a way that doesn't sound bonkers. That I came looking for you and you walking into this cafe was chance, maybe, but I had put all my bets on it. I knew in my gut it would work. Even if I had to come back a million times.

You stop laughing, lean across the table, and get your nose close to mine. I almost lean away out of instinct, remind why I'm here, and lean in closer so the tips of our noses snog for a brief second. You don't pull away either and we stay like that for a minute without words. Just sitting, connected.

"I believe you," you say in a husky way.

I grin and it pushes our noses closer, making the mash-up a little uncomfortable. Which gives me a really out-there idea. "I wish we weren't in public," I say.

You sigh, your breath smells like caramelized sugar and it's delicious. "Why is that?"

"Because," I lick my lips. "then I would ask if I could kiss you."

"Ask anyway."

"I..." can't do it. Not in public. Not with the owner who we've both already offended looking on. No way.

"The owner's gone to run an errand. I said we could wait. We're alone."

"Oh..."

"So what are you waiting for?"

"Nothing," I say and lean in, mouth barely parted.

Our lips meet and it's utter blistering joy.

Heat bursts like a bomb inside my mouth, my belly, my heart. I feel as though I'm glowing. Embers of excitement washed in the fuel of relief. I could swear the snow outside is melting and trees are turning green. Flowers blooming. Life bursting forth from every nook and crevice of the room. The summer harvest is coming.

You pull away and the winter crashes back into me. Leaves turn, fall, die in wet gutters. The sky goes from bright white to cynical dark grey. The rain comes. The snow. Ice clings to everything, and I am back in my isolation again.

I look longingly into the black ovals of your eyes. Each is a dancing kaleidescope of light from icicles, paper lanterns, the glowing wood stove fire behind me. Each light twirls in perfect alignment, following choreographed steps weaving a masterful spell. But I can't tell if it's being cast on me or you.

Which of us is the better liar? Me with my innocence or you with whatever your secret magic is?

Your soft, delicate hand with bones like porcelain reaches out across the worn out slats of wood. I reach back, my thick hand careful not to crush you. You smile up at me with your stencil thin ruby red lips. I smile back, my thick bottom lip pursing and pouting like it does whenever I'm aroused.

Your laugh is the bashful giggle of women in your culture. Mine is throaty and deep, a wave thrashing against a jagged volcanic coast. It becomes the roll of thunder in an oncoming storm tumbling land-ward off the coast of Kaneohe Bay. A crashing clapping boom of mirth from the throat of my people generations back.

You stand. "Let's get out of here."

"But we haven't even ordered?"

"So?"

"I..." don't have an answer to that.

"It seems rude?" you peak an elegant eyebrow at me.

I nod slowly.

"Besides, I already apologized," you explain.

I start, shocked.

"What?" you huff, a hand on your hip as you pull me up from the chair.

"That's not the Mikata I recall."

You blush and run thin fingers through your silken midnight hair. "The Mikata you remember is two years changed, Sammy."

I nod. "And so is the Sammy you knew. It's just Sam now."

You turn toward the door without pause. "I can tell. You look different."

"Different bad?" I pull on a strand of my hair as if tugging it will make it long enough to hide behind. Old habit. Back when I had light brown hair down to my elbows, a place to hide was the only thing that matted mess was good for.

"Not bad. Still beautiful," you say gently.

I blush deeper, tug more.

"Stop it," you say in a firm voice that stills me.

I put my hands in my pockets instead, hunching my shoulders.

"And bundle up. It is winter out there, you know."

"I know," I say and think: yeah, but it's summer in my heart.

We step outside. There is a blast of freezing air that whisks the warmth right off my skin. Below zero Celsius, without a doubt. And despite all the warmth inside, I'm snapped back to reality. To the winter. To the reason I've come "on vacation" to Otaru.

I steal a glance at you. Our eyes meet for a brief second and I realize I have no idea what you're thinking.

The cold is a reminder to be awake and wary. The snow, a reminder of how cold I behaved in leaving you. A warning that I may not be able to melt the ice that could be packed around your heart, for all I know. It's not like I ever asked.

Even now, I've made no mention of my intentions. No motion at apologizing. Nothing. I'm playing cool tourist with a clear record. A block of ice in my own way. It's not on purpose, I just can't help but feel like you already know my heart. But that's not fair. Maybe not even possible. I try to catch your eye again to see what you might be thinking. But you've put your hood up and all I see is fur collecting bits of snow. I tuck my scarf into the collar of my coat, and shivering pull up my own hood. I think to reach for the crook of your arm, but the wind is sucking the warmth from my fingers like the summer sun strips layers of a popsicle. So, instead of reaching out, I stuff both hands into my pockets.

You glance my way, eyes hidden under your halo of fur and shadow. But I see enough to see your playful grin as you pull a hand from your pocket, reach out, and tuck your hand into the crook of my arm. The warmth of summer returns, flushing my hands and cheeks. Bolstered by the warmth, I clamp my arm down on your gloved hand, hoping my warmth seeps to your fingers through all our combined layers. I feel a squeeze back and think maybe, in a metaphorical sense, it has. Smiling across at you through a thin wisp of snow, I promise myself again that I'm not going to just drift about anymore.

"I owe you an apology," I say quietly.

You don't miss a beat. "Yes, you do. Douzo." Meaning, "go ahead" or better translated in this case: "please."

"I'm sorry."

I feel your fingers tighten through the down and polyester shell of of my coat. "I forgave you two years ago."

"Why?" I miss a step and fall behind you ever so slightly.

You pull me back up to speed. "Isn't it obvious?"

"It's not," I admit.

Your laugh is like warm oil poured into my aching, wind battered ears. "I love you too."

Silence fills the gap between us. It's not uncomfortable and empty, but safe and full. A wholeness that the snow, the wind, the chill can't steal. You move to close the space and lay your head on me. If I were a handful of centimeters taller, it'd be my chest and you'd feel my heartbeat hammering for you. But it's not and so maybe you feel nothing but my bones. The structure that holds me up. I think that's pretty fitting.

"I have my own confession to make," you whisper into my armpit.

"What is it?" I say, unworried.

"The thing about my brother getting married. I lied."

"Your brother isn't getting married?"

"He is, but it's not why I came."

"Then why?"

"Because the hostel manager rang me the day you booked your trip."

"You knew I was looking for you?"

"No. I only hoped."

I breathe out, relieved I wasn't the only one making wildly poor choices based on flimsy thin dreams. "It's okay."

"There's more. I told my brother I'd bring you."

"Hm?" I hum, confused.

"He wants to meet you. All of them do."

"Your family? But...Mikata. The marriage thing – it was a joke. I'm not ready for..." I stammer, the chill of worry creeping in through narrow cracks in my defenses. The last thing I'm ready for is standing up to a traditional family and explaining that their beautiful daughter wants to marry me of all people. Foreign. Poor. Not a man.

You pull away, head shaking. "That's not the reason."

"What then?"

"My brother can explain better than I can."

"Okay," I give in rather than fight. What harm can it do? "Let's go."

We walk to the front of an old ragged warehouse right on the other side of the ocean. Across the bridge to our left, a road leads to the port where boats will be loaded and unloaded in the morning. For now, the town is closing up shop. I glance at my watch. It's barely past four thirty and already the sun is setting. I look up and stare at the warehouse doors. The wood is peeling, the lock is rusted on. On the three floors above our heads, all the windows are boarded up.

"This place looks shut down," I say as if you haven't noticed.

"It's not," you say and approach a smaller door I hadn't noticed off to the right.

The door creaks open on wobbly rusted hinges. From inside, there is the surprising salty savory smell of yakiniku – grilling meat on an open fire. A gentle light smoke wafts toward us, sucked outside by the draft our opening this door has created. Across the darkness, there is the sound of shuffling and a jumble of sounds I know must be Japanese. I don't catch a word of it. You go ahead of me, boldly strutting across to the dim orange glow tucked in a far corner. The hard clack of your heavy heeled boots echoes across the room. My shoes, softer soled, tacka-tack along at a shorter, quicker pace. Even from the echoes, I can tell you are confident and I am nervous.

"Mikata!" calls a sharp, middle-range voice. I can't tell if it's your brother or not. We met once in that legendary summer, but both face and voice disappeared from my memory like a photograph left out in the sun for years.

"Hai! Mikata da. Samu mo iru yo." you announce both of our presences.

"Kuru zo." Come.

We go hand in hand toward the fire, crossing complaining slats of ancient blackened wood. Several sofr spots threaten to give out under us. I trip right as you swing gaily into the firelight. It bursts upon your skin like a wave, lighting up every feature with a splash, foaming away in dim shadows. Your hood falls back, face revealed in full for the first time since our mutual confession. Cheeks cherry red, lips smiling, eyes staring straight ahead.

I follow your gaze to a short guy with long black hair down to the elbows. Rivers of blue-black that end in shores of bleached white blond. Piercing blue eyes that must be contacts stare ice cold, not at you, but me. I look down at my shoes and notice how dirty they are. How tired and worn.

"You're late," Makoto says in a sharp British accent.

"Un, gomen'na," you say in a traditionally mannish way. Claiming strength in the face of Makoto and the rest of these...cronies, I can't help but think.

I feel my confidence shrink even more when Makoto takes a step in my direction. "Sammy, is it?"

"S-sam," I manage to croak out.

A hand clamps on the soft spot of my neck like jaws of a pit bull. I'm worried Makoto will never let go until I've bled out. "Mikata explained?"

"Uh," I say and look to you for instruction, but you've left my side to grill skewers of meat like we're at a friend's Sunday picnic. I blink, shrink even further into myself, and shift. Makoto's hand tightens on my neck and I inadvertently twitch. Pressure points.

"No. Of course she didn't. Look," Makoto uses the grip to steer me away from the fire. Away from the warmth that had just begun to thaw my fingers, nose, toes. Away from the light and into the darkness of the decaying room.

I sniffle and my nose is filled with mildew and mold. Despite being cold and scared and alone, I'm reminded of that jam-packed rush hour train two years ago from Harajuku to Shibuya the day we first met. The smell is almost identical, and I remember not my disgust at the weather – but my delight at having you in my arms.

"I want you to protect her," Makoto's voice bites my ear, and I'm back in the warehouse again, shivering.

"Okay," I say. That doesn't sound so bad. It also doesn't require a warehouse and secret meetings in the dark. *So what else is going on?* I don't have the bravery to ask.

"It's complicated," Makoto goes on for my benefit.

"H-how so?"

"Mikata's in trouble."

"With?" I'm thinking credit card debit. A bad bet. Things I can't do anything about.

"Arranged marriage."

"I..." can't believe what I'm hearing.

"So here's the plan. You take her to...where is it your from? Hawaii?"

"Honolulu to be exact."

"Good. You take her to Honolulu. You can get married there?"

"Y-yes."

"Then do. After, send her back with the...how do you say...the receipt?"

"Certificate."

"She shows it to her dad. The arrangement is off. Nothing he can do. Then, you two do what you want. Stay here. Move to Hawaii. Don't care."

"I..." still can't believe what I'm hearing. "You want me to marry Mikata so that she doesn't have to marry someone else?"

"Yes. A real bad guy. You protect her. Mamoru no tame. You understand?"

Literally the words mean: for the benefit of protecting. "Yes," I say.

"Good. Then you agree?"

I can think of a million reasons why I should say no. And a million reasons why this will never work. But I can also think of a million reasons why I want to say yes – only, I wish it could have been more romantic. Candles and roses instead of a dirty old warehouse and mildew mixed with meat smoke. But here I am and there you are, across the darkness, flipping over little skewers of meat dripping in thick brown sauce. One of them catches fire and your lips, lit from underneath by the blue flame, pucker so beautifully and blow it out like you are kissing the air.

And the flame you kill on the meat jumps to my heart and burns me up. All I want in the world is for your lips to blow on my like that. Like you are kissing my flaming heart. I try to imagine myself saying no, returning to my hostel alone. And in the morning, trudging solo through knee deep snow to Otaru station, boarding a plane, and stepping out into the tropical balmy warmth of Hawai'i without your hand in mine.

And I can't do it. I can't see it. I can't say no. I can't drift off and disappear from your life. Even if it means the most ridiculous situation in all the world – I'd rather say yes than lose you.

"Yes," I say finally.

"Yes?" Makoto repeats with a piercing look. It goes right through me like a blade of blue ice.

"Yes."

"Then you are family," Makoto grabs me and wraps me in a hug that I don't expect. I stumble, foot catching on a loose floorboard, and bring us to the ground. The ruckus stirs the pot of others at the fire cooking. There's shouts in Japanese, and I don't need to know the words to know their angry. Feet rushing. The sound of...is that metal? Chains? Guns being cocked?

And then, it hits me.

"Your family… you are yakuza," I blather stupidly, thinking only: real bad people.

Makoto laughs, slapping me across the back and pushing off my spine to stand up. "Dai jou bu, dai jou bu!" he calls, saying everything is fine. "We are not bad like you think. We protect our own from the bad ones. You understand?"

"Yes," I say shakily, but I'm unsure.

"Good," and Makoto calls out more stuff in rushed (angry?) Japanese.

The ruckus of weapons and feet rushing to kill me stop. More rushed Japanese with loads of slang that I don't catch a word of. Everyone seems to go back to what they were doing. Eating, cooking, drinking, muttering about killing people or something.

I lay there, shivering. Terrified.

Makoto stands over me, reaching down. Beside him, you've appeared in a glowing glory that makes my chest tighten. Gangsters or not, how could I have said no? Isn't this what I came here for? Isn't this everything I want?

"I want to protect you, Sammy," you said two years ago.

Maybe, I didn't know what that meant. Maybe I was too scared to ask. But now? I wouldn't have it any other way.

I take Makoto's hand and stand.

"I want to protect you, Mikata," I say, reaching for you.

You come easily into my arms, and we sink deep into an all-encompassing kiss like it's the most natural thing we could do. I can feel you smiling, sly and dark, against my lips. I press into you until I feel your teeth against mine. Our mouths pressed together are wet and hot and we are stuck together. Just like in Tokyo, mid-summer.

Everything is bliss.

# A Horrible Match

## A Short Dark Fantasy

### Rei Rosenquist

# A Romantic Vinette

The roses in the garden were dead. Nadi left them that way as a reminder.

Blame it on the madness. No, not madness. An awareness. A state of being.

Nadi saw people like tentacles...no, less creepy. Arms, or um. Something soft. Yes, yarn with loose threads fraying out. Each thread was its own unique color. More colors than the rainbow, complex and beautiful.

But, there's an ugly side. All these...threads writhe. Alive and reaching, got tangled with others on passing, accidentally touching, brief eye-contact. Average people thought it meant nothing, those moments. Only, Nadi knew the truth. Every interaction changed a person's crisp clear color. Warped it. Muddied it forever.

Ever since the electrical storm, Nadi couldn't unsee these tentacles... No, threads. Lines of energy. That's all.

Couples and groups of individuals existed like color wheels. Some people had it better off, their colors were complimentary blues or greens, so when touching and morphing, the resultant blend was something somewhat delightful. Others however, were mismatched and grotesque. Those people would lean into one another, laughing, sharing a hug or a brief kiss. And Nadi couldn't help but cringe.

That was why the roses are dead.

To serve as a reminder.

Because George the gardener's thread was a stunningly ugly color. So ugly it made Nadi want to call the threads tentacles. Something slimy and squicky. Something to get far, far away from.

Even thinking about George's tentacle made Nadi sick. So, she planned to send him away with some terrible excuse just to get rid of the garish hue. Something about taking a very pricey holiday. After the prescribed time, Nadi would call George up and say they just couldn't pay for a gardener anymore.

Not that Nadi didn't love everything George did in the garden.

No, no, no. Not at all.

It was just George's color was all wrong.

That, and the way he looked at her through the window when he didn't think she noticed. A leery, ugly-toned look. Like she was a piece of meat, and he was devastatingly hungry. And, truth be told, the longer George had been working for her, the more unsettling their interactions had become. The way he hung around close to the pathways anytime Nadi ventured out, pruning a vine that didn't need pruning. The way he came up with innocent-enough excuses to touch her wrist, her arm. The way he went to brush hair away from her face, claiming a wayward breeze that wasn't there.

Working up the courage, Nadi approached George on New Year's Eve with the fake story.

"You work so hard. I mean, just look at the Shakespearean section of the garden! Beautiful." Nadi gushed, trying hard to cover the terror that George would refuse to stay away in the supposed absence.

But George, despite the hideous chartreuse thread glaring in Nadi's eye, acted cordial and kind. "See you in a couple weeks, I will?"

"Of course," Nadi lied, scared to say the truth.

"Just telly when you're back in town, love. And I'll nip right on over."

"Of course, of course."

George wrote down a telephone number and Nadi folded it neatly, pretending to preserve it. The second George was out of sight and that god-awful color disappeared around the bend that led into town, Nadi crumpled the number up and thrown it in a rubbish bin. That rubbish bin got taken out by the night staff that evening.

Gone for good. And good riddance.

Late that night, Nadi breathed a sign of relief and sadness, leaning out the window at the slowly rotting garden. It was a shame, though, wasn't it? Letting the garden go to waste like that. Letting the plants just run wild.

Two weeks later, Nadi was enjoying the peace and quiet when the door bell rang.

"Tobe, someone's at the door," Nadi called, not wanting to answer it.

With Nadi's gift, answering calls had become a tangled affair these days. Blinking, trying not to be touched by the reaching tentacles of a stranger, making vague excuses to lean away. It made Nadi look more crazy than sane. "Batty witch," Nadi was afraid the neighborhood kids would start to whisper. Or worse.

*Possessed.*

Implying Nadi's mind and actions were not by choice. But some other will using Nadi like a meat puppet. The thought was horrifying and Nadi discarded it instantly. Instead, around about the same time George had left, Nadi hired on Tobe to help answer calls. Avoiding George's inevitable return may or may not have been secret motivation.

Tobe wasn't exactly a house servant, per say. More like an old college kid in need of a room. In exchange for rent, Tobe agreed to do odds and ends around the grounds. Nadi didn't mind the help or the company. Tobe's color was a nice powder blue-grey and somehow Tobe kept those pretty tentacles tucked, rolled up, and under control.

"Visitor!" Tobe called up from the front door.

"Who is it?" Nadi huffed, annoyed.

People weren't supposed to know you were home when you had a door person. Door people were supposed to make up inarguable excuses like "The master of the house is indisposed at the moment. Completely unavailable."

That's how it went in stories. Why not in real life?

"Nadi will be right down," Tobe said in a loud tone.

Worst door person, ever. At least Tobe's tenacle was a nice powder blue color. The color in Nadi's mind of good intentions. Poor execution, but a good heart. Not like George with that awful color and those muddled intentions. Tobe was easy to read, authentic and straightfoward.

Nadi trudged down the spiral staircase in a swooping black dressing gown. Tobe stepped out of the way to reveal none other than:

"George." Nadi's voice was a shocked breath.

He was wearing his gardening gloves, leering at her with a big knowing grin. "Begging your pardon. But the garden looks something awful. I was just passing through and couldn't help but notice."

The wall around Nadi's place should have kept him from noticing. His excuse was see-through. But before Nadi could get the words out, George's tentacle lashed out and wrapped around her middle. Nadi wanted to bat it off, to run and scream like a spider had jumped at her chest. But, she didn't dare. What would George think? Nadi didn't want to find out. Besides, the neighbors would be up in arms. This was a quiet part of town. People didn't go screaming for no reason. She forced a smile on her lips.

"I was just about to ring you!" Nadi lied out of fear.

"Well. It's about time," George said in a way that implied he'd known the holiday had been a lie all along. He winked by way of saying, "all's forgiven now."

"Why not get back to it? Because you're right. The roses are just awful."

George didn't say a thing, turned, and trotted off into Nadi's rose bed, clippers swinging.

Tobe shifted awkwardly. "There's something funny happening."

Nadi looked down at the ugly chartreuse tentacle wrapped like a rope around her middle. It completely clashed with Nadi's bright orange-gold. Tobe shouldn't be able to see it. No one could. They'd all think George was just a kindly gentleman and Nadi was a silly old dame.

"What's funny?" Nadi asked, voice shaking.

Tobe eyed George as he walked away. "It's just him coming back like that. After you sent him away for good."

"I didn't exactly send George away for good," Nadi admitted.

"You ought to have."

The tentacle around Nadi's waist tightened. Not horribly aggressive yet. Only slightly for now. A reminder of what could come next. The fear was lowkey, a fluttering in Nadi's belly.

*So that is what people call "butterflies," is it. Feels like a nausea-vice.*

"I think I'd rather not," Nadi said to make the feeling subside.

"You should though," Tobe turned for the stairs up to the renters, then paused and shuddered. "Something about that George guy gives me the creepies."

Outside, George was hard at work on the roses. Already, the garden looked better. George noticed Nadi, straightened, flashed a grin and winked. The tentacle snuggled in close around Nadi's belly. The ugly vice that first felt like nausea had turned warm and oh so nice.

Nadi smiled back, heart feeling huge.

Tobe was wrong. There was nothing creepy about this.

George's timing was coincidentally perfect. Nadi had missed him.

It was good to have him and his funky color back around.

He wasn't a perfect match, but he wasn't all bad.

"No one is ever all bad," Nadi said out loud, hoping to get Tobe off her back.

"Doesn't mean it's not a bad match."

"I think you're right," Nadi said.

But still, something stopped her from going out and chasing George away. Most people would have called it a lack of resolve, feminine weakness, or an inability to stand up for herself. Years of programming. But Nadi knew the truth this time. She'd been trapped simply by letting George in. And, it'd take a lot more cleverness than just admitting the problem to get herself back out of this mess.

Nadi looked down at the clashing chartreuse tentacle around her middle. It wasn't going to give up easily, but it'd let go eventually. Nadi gave the tentacle a gentle stroke, coming up with a plan.

Tobe eyed her curiously.

Nadi smiled back, touching her own wrist, her arm, brushing hair from her cheek from a breeze that wasn't blowing. She stood tall despite the tentacle wrapped tight around her middle.

"Soon enough, Tobe, he'll be gone for good."

The resolve alone gave her a little room to breathe, the tentacle uncoiling ever so slightly, as if it knew it's time was already up.

* * *

# A SIMPLE LOVE STORY

A SHORT FANTASY BY

# REI ROSENQUIST

*One*

I was twenty-one; you were twenty-two. We were both out of our element in a strange place.

Our presence in Venice, Italy was neither coincidence nor fate. It was a summer enrichment program arranged by both our colleges under the same guise: 'archaeological studies.' It set up kids like us for this kind of world experience. A brief glimpse into the other. For those eager enough, it was a brief chance. A glimpse at what friendship, community, love could be. We never expected it to work. Maybe that's why it did.

I came off the plane with a teddy bear in my arms. You had on headphones and wouldn't look at anyone. We sat side-by-side in the food court and chewed on rubbery chicken nuggets because there was nowhere else to go. I set my teddy bear in my lap. You slid your headphones half off but didn't look up. I held up an odd shaped nugget and wrinkled my nose.

You leaned in, our eyes meeting. "Nobody's making you eat it," were your first softly accented words. A linguistic birth in my mind.

"I'll feel guilty if I waste it."

"I see."

Our smiles met, equally exhausted from a day of luggage, airports, and customs.

"It's better in honey mustard," you said and pointed at a little pot of sauce right beside my elbow that I'd somehow missed.

"Where'd that come from?" I asked. "Did you bring it over?"

"Sure," you smiled crookedly like you knew something I didn't.

I took the offering and dipped the corner of the cheap meat into it. The sauce was bright yellow-orange, and I couldn't tell what the flavor was supposed to be other than the bad kind of science that makes cheap imitations of good things.

I wrinkled my nose. "It's not helping."

We both laughed outright.

"Ok kids! Let's load it up!" our Italian chaperon called with a lack of an accent that made me think they weren't really Italian at all.

When we got up, it was at the same time. I cradled my teddy bear. You moved to pull the headphones back on.

"What bus you on?" I asked quickly.

"A," you said and disappeared behind music again.

I looked down at my seat assignment. A34. I suddenly hoped that was the seat next to you.

*Two*

3 4 and 35 A. That was you and I. We sat elbow to elbow while the countryside of Italy slid by. The airport was a surprising distance from what I thought Venice looked like. We crossed low rolling hills, passed by old houses, and dropped into the heart of a city-city. I looked out the window, disappointed.

"Where are all the canals?" you asked before I could.

I pressed my forehead to the window and let my breath fog it up. "I don't know."

"Do you think the photos are exaggerated?"

I chuckled pessimistically. "Maybe. I mean, Paris isn't exactly like all Eiffel Tower, Louvre, Arc de Triumph, catacombs, and done."

"True," you sounded as disappointed as I felt.

Which made me readjust myself, letting my arm press against your warm skin the way kids do that feels like it means something. "That'd suck," I said importantly.

You sagged. "Yeah, right?"

"We'll just have to do our own thing!" I teased.

"Yeah, we can make it what we want it to be." You had said it nonchalant, but it sounded like more.

I looked up and your brown eyes were alight like we'd just shared a big secret. I fidgeted, hand automatically covering my wristband in a careful way. No way you know my big secret, I thought. No way.

Outside, the bus crossed out of the city limits and climbed over a bridge. The unexpected metropolis melted away, replaced by water everywhere. It shimmered and glittered and looked full of light. The old buildings rose tan, brown, and gold all around us. We half-watched the world outside, half-watched each other's eyes. In a few more moments, old Venice swallowed us.

"Oh! Here it is," I whispered to myself, inadvertently close to your ear.

You nodded like I was talking to you. "So it is."

I smiled because I liked the idea of us sharing secrets.

You smiled back and I felt safer than I ever have.

The Italian-with-no-accent chaperon came on the intercom and made announcements about the city, the hotel, curfew. As the bus pulled into the underground parking lot on the edge of one of the biggest canals, the chaperon gave more instructions. Everyone got up at the same time, clambered off the bus, and filled a lobby that was kind of cheap and dingy.

I turned to you while we waited in line to get our keys. "Hope we have rooms near each other."

Again, your eyes sparkled with a mischievous warmth. "Me too."

The chaperon was about to hand me a key, fumbled, and handed me a different one. "This is you."

You held out your key toward me, eyes sparkling. "317, you?"

I looked down and gasped with surprise. "319! What do you know."

We headed to the elevator together, fingers touching as we both pressed the up arrow.

"Did you make this happen?" I joked.

You blushed dark red. "What? That's silly."

My face fell and I looked away. Caught up in our fun, I'd gone and opened my big mouth. I'd forgotten fact number one: we weren't the same thing. You were a normal person, and I was a Binder. It had been a big risk to send me out alone to another country. I had no idea what kind of binding I might accidentally do if I panicked.

"Stay calm and keep to yourself." Mama had said at the airport.

"I will, I promise." I'd said earnestly. I had meant it. But we never guessed what I'd do if I met another Binder. Why would we? It was impossible.

The elevator came and we stood in it, side by side and silent. I watched my face frowning in the mirror. I was worried about having rooms so close. Worried, more than anything, that I'd slip up again. You were cute and cool, and talking to you felt easy. I wanted to be real, honest, all of me. But I couldn't, and I knew it. I needed to be careful.

And yet, leaving the elevator all I could think was: what if being careful makes you think I'm weirdo, and you ignore me?

"You okay?" You asked, leaning against your door.

"Um, yeah."

You frowned. "I don't believe you."

"I'm tired," I lied, and felt my stomach sink. You wouldn't like me now.

"Sleep it off."

I nodded, thinking that was you saying goodbye.

You flashed a toothy grin. "You'll need lots of rest if we're going to do our own thing. Remember?"

$$\mathcal{T}hree$$

We had no time.

The tour ran us to the bone. Everyday was the same. Wake at 5 am, hapless shower, and have an hour to eat. Breakfast was cheap coffee (brewed through a sock I swear) or flavorless from-concentrate orange juice, supermarket bread, two different colors of the same cheese, and mushy fruit. After b-fast, eight hours of touring. Break to eat. Another eight hours of touring. Break to eat. Do the prescribed journaling that made this trip credits for the "301 International Explorations" class. Sleep. Repeat.

Lunch and dinner were both "included", but that was a lie. It meant that the tour bus stopped at some ultra expensive restaurant/tourist trap and we were expected to pay whatever the menu said. Plus big tip. Menus all being in Italian, I couldn't read a word. But I could see the Euros I was expected to fork over. Upwards of the equivalent of $30 USD a meal.

I started poaching cheap non-perishable foods from the b-fast buffet pretty quick. I caught you in line ahead of me on the seventh day. We shared that same look from the bus, when we both thought Venice might be a let-down of ideals.

You picked a pasty barely-brown roll and held it up. It was so thin of substance, it could have been from an American fast food chain. "Good shit, eh?" you winked.

"Oh yeah," I wanted to wink back, but I've never been good at winks. Both my eyes closed momentarily.

You were smiling broadly in my face when they opened back up. "I'm pretty sick of this."

"Me too."

You leaned in. Our elbows touched. We gasped in unison like we'd been electrically shocked.

"What do you say we ditch the tour today?"

I fidgeted. I burned to say yes, but wasn't that the definition of not being careful?

You leaned in closer. "We said we'd do it. It'll be an adventure."

My stomach fluttered and I felt hot all over. Wasn't that exactly why I'd come? To try something new? "Ok," I said without thinking.

You plotted out a plan that sounded like you'd been thinking about it for days. We'd both go to the bathroom right when the chaperon was getting everyone on the bus. Each bathroom on the first floor had a window that we could climb out without much trouble. I hadn't remembered a window there, but then, I hadn't spent much time in the bathroom either. So, riding the same whim that made me say "yes", I decided to trust you. Part of me secretly thought: even if there were no windows, I can bind one for both of us; no sweat.

When the chaperon came making the rounds, we made brief eye contact. You went first. "Oh, I gotta use the bathroom."

"Oh! Me too!" I hopped up.

Trusting to the old cliché: girls never go to the bathroom alone. I wasn't "exactly" a girl, legally speaking. But only somebody who took a look at my passport knew that. So, this should work. And sure enough. When I hopped up, nobody batted an eye. The chaperon didn't even pause. It was that easy.

In the bathroom, there was a window like you said there was. A little gateway that led conveniently to an alleyway that was clear and clean. It felt like magic for as easy as it was. But then, I had to remind myself: I was the only Binder I'd ever known. Chances of randomly finding one on a school tour in Italy? Zero to none.

Outside, we stood side by side, confronted with choices. All of Venice, open and waiting. I did something daring and reached my hand out for yours. To my dismayed glee, you took it. Our fingers interlaced. I squeezed your hand; you squeezed back. Nobody had ever squeezed back. Standing facing a new city, new streets, new adventures, and new fears, I thought – this! This is all I want from the world.

"Where do we go first?" you asked, sounding a little unsure.

"Let's follow the moon," I said and pointed up.

Above our heads, it was a faint sliver against the sky. We were a few days past the new moon, and this sliver was the first sign of the next phase. A new chance.

I wondered if you'd even see it. Most people didn't notice the moon during the day, but I always knew where it would be. Whenever I saw the moon, I thought of grandma and grandpa. I thought of my heirloom wristband, passed down for generations. Burned into the leather was an intricate insignia of a round knot. Its being there was a part of my truest identity. Whenever I thought of it, I thought of binding.

I wanted to bind a you to be with me forever. How silly, I thought and moved to walk.

You followed my lead, and off we went, step for step. I realized as we walked, I had never walked anywhere with anyone. Our hands linked, I felt the beginnings of a shadow peeling away from me. The shadow of isolated despair.

We walked until we were lost. The alleys twisted and curved. We'd come out to an intersection, facing the exactly opposite direction from which we'd set off. We'd turn back, take another route, and never come out at the same place. It was like weaving a tangled web, one street corner and plaza and canal bridge at a time.

We sat in a huge square around midday and unpacked our lunch. That cheap continental breakfast spread in miniature. It was a bounty of underwhelming, under-nourishing foods. But it was free, so it still tasted like a win. I tossed you a bruised apple and you traded me a flimsy roll. We broke a triangle of oil-cheese-product in half and split it.

"Did you grab something else to eat?" I said, belly growling.

"Nope. But we could get a latte. This is Italy after all."

I liked the idea. "Okay."

We found ourselves standing outside a cafe faced with a menu that didn't make much sense. We kept flipping pages to no effect. You pointed at a long list of words. "Funny, I thought I'd understand this."

"Me too. Dumb, huh?" I tried to joke, but did feel dumb. I ran a hand through my hair, feeling the stubble of the newly shaved side. It was kind of an experimental design. When I felt insecure, I found my hand returning to it. A reminder I didn't fit with others.

"It looks great."

"What does?" I stared at the menu, but then realized you weren't looking at it.

"Your hair. I love the purple. Can I?" you reached for my fuzz.

"Um."

You recoiled so easily. "I'm sorry, it's just so cool. Like you're so..."

I held my breath, filling in the blank with lots of things. "Prissy, girlish, effeminate". All synonymous with "unacceptable" or worse, "wrong". I braced myself, leaning ever so slightly away. Like a bit of air between us could protect me.

"--you!"

"What?"

"Yeah, like, that's it. You're so you. Unique, cool. I like you. A lot. Also, all those colors?! Your hair's so rad."

I blushed, recalling why I'd dyed it. My teddy bear collection back home. Their fur was all colors of the rainbow on purpose. Reminders that everyone could be different. Those colored bears were my memories, too. Pink cotton candy of my first county fair, blue crystal clear sky of sailing in the bay, purple lavender flowers in my grandparents' yard. The tattered old silver teddy bear back in my room was particularly special. Fur the color of the moon. That teddy bear had come to Venice because it was the only one who understood me. Until now.

"Okay," I leaned my head toward you, "you can touch."

You ran fingers through my hair and then laid your head on top of mine, sighing. You were a just few inches taller than me. We fit together.

"Do we still want coffee?" I asked.

"Naw, let's see keep wandering," you said and we took off again, two kids lost in a city but found in each other's easily given affection. Feeling so full of heart, it wasn't difficult to ignore the grumbling in our bellies.

## Four

The sinking sun cast elongated shadows, and I started to worry about our adventure. We twisted through what felt like the same streets a dozen times. I began recognizing water taxi stops and the cafe we'd stopped in front of. The hollow spot in my stomach, I realized, was both hunger and a knot. Because for all the sites I'd come to recognize, I never once saw our hotel.

"Have you seen our hotel?" I asked you, trying to be nonchalant.

You shrugged, unworried. "Nope. But I'm hungry, aren't you?"

"Yeah, but..."

"Look, pizza!" you pointed at a cafe I swear wasn't there a second ago.

"Hey, that wasn't--"

"You like pizza?" you cut in.

"Well yeah, but did you--"

"Let's get some," you winked obviously.

I felt flush at the sight of it. The clearest sign of our secret companionship. Whatever it was based on, binding or not, I wanted more of it. What the hell, I thought. We could figure everything out later. For now, it was okay to keep wandering. "Okay!"

We walked in and sat without trying to read the menu. When the server came over and spoke to us in broken English, we didn't even flinch. You pointed at the first thing on the list and I giggled, nodding. The server smiled, nodded, and brought us free samples of wine. We drank and waited for whatever we'd ordered.

It was a simple cheese and tomato pizza and it came out steaming. We tucked in, gobbled it down, and for some reason got another sample of wine. We drank that glass down, too. The server presented us with the bill. Turns out those weren't samples.

We frowned and dug in our pockets, counting and recounting every last coin we had. It was just enough. We forked over all our cash and stared at one another.

"Oops. That was kinda pricey," you said, sheepish.

"Yeah."

You reached for my hand anyway. "I guess I should have been more careful, huh?"

I took your palm in mine and laughed at our pile of money on the table. "Yeah, serves us right for not checking."

You shook your head like you meant something else. Making me think, again, maybe you'd pulled that cafe to us. But, you couldn't be a Binder. It was impossible.

We got up, leaving all our resources on the table. Sans cash, the world felt bigger and meaner than it had before. The pit in my stomach wasn't gone but cluttered with food and alcohol. I glanced at you as we headed for the door. You looked the same as me. Darkly worried. Is this how adventures end? Is this what being an adult is like? You try and come up not short, but just shy of feeling right?

"Where to now?" you sounded deflated.

I looked up at the sky. It was dark enough to see stars. "I'm tired."

"Me too."

"Let's go back."

"You know the way?"

"Sure. Let's see."

## Five

We wandered streets, me checking a free map I'd snatched from some tourist trap, and you checking what you claimed were the stars. I didn't believe you and kept sneaking glances at your face. To see if you were trying to bind the hotel to us. That'd be a huge spell and I didn't think even I could do it. Even if I needed to.

Finally, you stopped at a corner between two alleyways and you pointed. "Let's go left."

"Left? But that's--" and I couldn't get "a dead end" out before you grabbed my hand and pulled me through it.

To my shock, it wasn't a wall at all. We stood in a wide closed space. There were pretty orange glass lights hanging every few feet, making the hallway not ominous but long.

"Whoa!" I gasped. That was definitely magic.

"We'll take the tunnels underground. It's a shortcut."

I didn't move, too shocked. You had to be a Binder.

"Don't worry. I have a plan."

I felt glued to the ground. It was impossible. Everything grandma and grandpa had taught me. Everything I knew about history of Binders. We were rare and the odds were too slim.

You stopped and gave me that look. The one from the b-fast line, from the bus. It was -- I know realized -- more than friendly. It was familiar. Like we already knew each other. Like you saw through my colored hair and moon colored teddy bear into the truth. That I was different, terrified, and in hiding. You moved the hand in mine to my arm.

"It's okay. I know what you are."

I cringed. Every time anyone said that, they were wrong.

You leaned in. "We are all in hiding in our own way."

"We," I repeated. So, it was true.

You indicated my wristband. An heirloom, yes, but more than that. Under its intricate weave, the same pattern existed. But instead of a lone knot, the weave was tied around a very realistic depiction of the moon. The skin looked like a scar, but it'd always been there. The birthmark of a Binder. The mark was different for everyone, and it always indicated a Binder's true name. For me: Moon Binder.

"You too? For real?" I looked for your mark. Grandma had said that one day I'd find others. But, to be honest, I'd never believed her. I felt too alienated, too excluded, too alone to believe that anyone could ever know what it was like to be something nobody else had words for.

I looked down at the front frilly edge of my pink and blue skirt. Below that, my legs, muscular and full of hair. And I thought: that too. I'd lived a life of being critiqued, picked apart, told I was wrong. How could I envision a world where even one person understood?

You pulled up the long brown hoodie sleeve you'd worn all day. Underneath was the marking. Your lines were black like a tattoo and the knot wove around a tree.

"Tree Binder," I whispered quietly, despite being in the safety of a magical hallway.

You tsked your tongue and pointed at the flowers on the ends of branches. They were giant white cups. "Magnolia. But you can call me Maggie."

"My parents call me Binny, but you can--" I fidgeted, realizing suddenly how awkward my family's nickname for me was. It only worked because I was the only Binder we knew. The only Binder, grandma had said, in all of North America. We were few and far between and so, going by Binny -- well, it had just made sense. But now, faced with another Binder...well, it felt pretentious.

You nodded deeply. "Binny it is. You are the only one, aren't you?"

"Yeah, aren't you?"

You shook your head and squeezed my hand. "How lonely you must be in the North."

I frowned. "How many are there in...uh...where are you from?"

"Peru. In my family, there are three. In all of Peru? I have no idea. A vast community."

I looked down, trying to imagine a community of Binders. I'd been raised to believe my skills were my own. I was trained to learn both the history of them and the art of their use. But binding was what grandpa called a "big magic". I should never use it for my own gain, but to help in situations that affected everything.

At twenty-one, I didn't even know what that looked like. So, I'd studied the arts of small things. Shifting air in a room, altering a thing's gravity (no bigger than a pencil), using my special Binder's sight to see things from the past through dreams. But never had I imagined actually doing anything worthy of being the only Binder in North America.

"Let's go back, hm?" you said.

I followed not because I couldn't figure out how to go back, but because I trusted you.

The hallway led in a twisty path, rising and falling across what I envisioned was the city above us. Or rather, outside of us. That was how binding actually worked. You didn't' so much change reality as pull other realities together. In some universe somewhere, grandma always said, there was a pencil floating right now. All I had to do was see that pencil and bring it here. Simple. I supposed in some other Venice, there was a tunnel underground. We walked through it easily, side by side, step for step.

When we got to a door, you stopped. "You got a story for us?"

"Me?!" I balked. "Why me?"

You laughed. "Because I'm no good at lying to normal people."

I recalled the times we'd interacted up until then. The headphones on the plane. The lack of talking in the b-fast line. The way you always leaned in when you spoke. "You don't talk, do you?"

You smiled and leaned in, even though we were clearly alone. "In a family of seven other Binders, you kind of never learn how to deal with outsiders."

And for the first time in my life, I knew what it felt like to be someone else's safe place. It was both comforting and scary. I leaned my head into your's. "Okay. I'll think of something."

Six

You had the tunnel come out in a small quadrangle where all the shops were closed for the day. We dawdled at the bottom of some stone steps with the hotel in our line of sight while I thought of a plan.

Correction. I thought of you, of magnolias, and of how I'd love to see Peru. I tried to think of a community of Binders so encompassing that I didn't know how to interact with common folk. I thought of what your school and education must have looked like. I thought of what family dinners would be like. I imagined a universe where I was you -- and then I stopped, getting scared I might accidentally pull a door into existence that would open onto that world.

After what felt like a half hour, you finally looked at me. The moon was a sliver and overhead and its reflection caught in the natural wetness of your eyes. Two glistening crescents staring back at me.

"You have something?"

"Not yet. Sorry, I was distracted."

"By?"

"Your life," I chuckled, feeling silly.

"Ah. It's not as glamorous as it seems."

"How do you mean?"

You said nothing but looked away.

"Maggie?" I touched your knee to pull your eyes back to me. They were black pools with no light as you stared at the steps below our feet.

"Our names," you began without looking up, "you know where they come from?"

"Our grandparents," I said, repeating the line I'd been taught. Magic always skipped a generation, waiting for the right host. Sometimes, it might skip two if there wasn't a suitable charge. I was fortunate in that I had three other siblings, none of whom were chosen. I knew this was how it worked, but not why. Like magic, it just *was*. Once the manifestation passed, both grandparents had a dream. And in that dream, the new Binder's name. Mine had come through a crescent moon hanging over water, like the one overhead.

"Sure, but why?"

"Because magic," I echoed what grandpa always said.

You tsked your tongue again. "Because gravity. One's place in the universes is defined by one's mass. The greater the name, the greater the game."

I recognized the line. It was taken from Forest, a famous Binder during the witch-hunt time period in America. It'd been said as an inspiration to those who were afraid of being burned. Forest had meant that anyone could be important. Or, so I thought.

"Forest meant the name magic chooses for us indicates our nature. The greater the name, the more influence over their world that Binder will have. It's not chance, Binny. It's fact."

I frowned at you. "But that would mean..."

"You have a great burden to bear."

I thought of all the time my grandparents spent training me, teaching me the ways of binding, teaching me to guard myself against the world, teaching me the ways of the universe. Science and an inquiring mind were not left out. Being a Binder was not to believe in sheer made-up fantasy. It was to believe, above all, in the truth of reality.

"You are made of the stars and many worlds," grandma would whisper and kiss my head before bed. I had always thought it was just a bindery thing to say. I'd never once imagined...

"You are the moon, Binny. And for earth, there's only one."

I knew what you were saying, but I was scared. And also, "But, if that's true, what about you, Maggie?"

"Our binding is spread among many. The community is strong, but with that comes less gravity per Binder. Mass divided into parts. When we stand together, we can change the shape of the world. But nothing in me is concentrated like it is in you. My abilities are light in comparison."

"In comparison to what?"

"To you. Everyone I've ever known is a satellite to the moon, or space junk flung far and wide."

I tried to think of the most outrageous thing I'd been taught. Changing wind patterns, turning tides, warming a fire from nothing, altering the course of a butterfly. Certainly, pulling an entire under-city hallway from another universe equated at least that. "But you got us back safe."

"A brief momentarily glitch in reality."

"And you put our rooms together, didn't you?"

A nod.

"And our seats on the bus." All the little things Maggie had done to make this moment happen were coming to me.

"Kid's play," you said and tried to bat my excitement away.

"Seems significant to me."

You smiled and nodded. "Yes, well. Maybe a single season for a flower is time enough to be bright and bold, and greatly loved."

I knew exactly what you meant. Not that you would die. But that your binding would never change the world, shift history, alter the course of a planetary body. Your magic, you believed, would be contained, brief and small. Your influence only ever a slow ripple from your hands into the lives of others. But suddenly, I saw in my mind's eye the image of a seed. I grabbed your shoulder suddenly. "No, Maggie. You have in you the makings of a tree."

You lifted your head up like I'd changed the force of gravity pushing you down. "I see," you said plainly. But I could hear something else behind your words. The hope of a new possibility.

I stood up. "I have a plan."

*Seven*

"What're you doing?" you asked as I tugged at what had been moments ago a small rip in my left pant leg.

I put the key away that I'd used to make the rip back into my pocket. "We need to look like we got lost."

"How do the holes help again?"

"We're gonna say we got mugged."

You didn't look convinced. "You're the talker, not me."

I used my key to wear down and rip two gaping holes, one in each knee. Then, I got up. "Let's go."

We climbed the steps, turned the last corner, and came up to the front of the hotel. There was no hunting party I was afraid would be there to meet with. In fact, everything looked normal. I took your hand and tried to look my part. You glanced at my face and tried to mimic it. To my displeasure, it was really stagy. I did a double-good effort for the two of us.

"To make it believable, we gotta run."

"Good idea."

We took off at full sprint. By the time we got to the hotel, we were visibly winded. It was easy to put on the rest of the character I needed to make this work. We burst into the lobby with a big bang. Inside, it was quiet and the not-quite-Italian chaperon was having a glass of wine and a cigarette. Upon spotting us, didn't even get up. "You two are back."

"We got mugged!" I blurted out.

"I bet," the chaperon took another drag.

You leaned into me and looked pathetic. You were most likely just trying to hide, nervous about talking to normal people. But the negative energy totally worked.

"Where do we call the police?" I cried.

The chaperon audibly scoffed, swirling wine. "You don't speak a word of Italian."

"But you do!"

"Passingly. But, I'm off the clock."

Is that a thing? Being off the clock as a tour guide? I frowned, trying to keep up the act. You put your head on my shoulder and sagged, whispering, "Is it working?"

I gave a little shake of my head.

The chaperon laughed. "Also, what's with the holes in your jeans? Those weren't there this morning."

I blushed, suddenly glad I hadn't used my binding to put them there. At least it was just a poorly executed lie and we couldn't get discovered for what we really were.

"We got mugged," I repeated with no conviction. I could feel you clinging to me. I put my arm around you and squeezed. If I couldn't lie good enough to get us out of trouble, I could at least be comforting.

"Look. Next time you two want to skip the tour, just say so. You ladies are both adults."

"Sorry," we both said in unison.

"You two lovebirds just go back to your room. No harm done."

We both burst into giggles, giddy from the high of having gotten away with something. The chaperon rolled eyes. We ducked out quickly. In the hotel hallway, we paused in the hollow space between our doors. The chaperon had planted the seed of an idea, but neither of us said a word. We just stood and stared.

Finally, you reached for my hand. I reached back.

"Do you want to--" I started, unsure what I wanted to ask. If you'd come to my room? If you'd stay with me? If we could remake the world together? If us meeting meant something bigger than just two people who, for a moment in time, understood each other? All I knew was I didn't want to let go.

You pulled away. "We might be of the same nature, Binny. But we are too different."

"I guess I see," but didn't really.

"A flower," you explained, "needs the sun. Not the moon. And you belong to the north and I to the south."

I thought then of our markings. Mine white, your's black. It was true. We were of two different worlds. Our chance meeting somewhere strange didn't change that. It had only given us the ability to see things a little differently, if only for a moment. If only for one day and one night.

You turned to leave, stopped, and turned back. "But do me a favor, will you?"

"Anything."

You smiled like you'd known I would say that. "Live up to your name. Be what you are, Binny."

"I will," I said.

We both turned to our own doors. Inside, I leaned against the cold wood of the door. The room was blank and dark, and I was alone. The same as at the beginning of our adventure. No, I thought. That was wrong. I had with me now the memory of your secret hallway, your smile, you in all its forms. A flower, beautiful and brief.

And suddenly, I felt less isolated than before. Less out of place. More known and understood. As if the sheer memory of our hands' embrace was a distant strength. A force that I could feel pulling me toward greatness even when you were far away. Just like the moon, I thought, and smiled. Held in a constant embrace by the massive gravity of the world. More than a mere magnolia flower, you held the seed to a tree of hope, branching and blooming forever inside of me.

Simple as that night may seem, I will never forget.

# She Sings Again

## A Short Fantasy

REI ROSENQUIST

*  *  *

*For Chick
A brave freeflying conure who may be lost,
But will never be forgot.*

*  *  *

The forest air is cold, crisp, and stuffed full of light.

It's no weather to bury a best friend in.

Yet, here Luminko is.

Bundled up, burial spade in one hand, the small swaddled body of a bird in the other.

Unwelcome sunlight slants through gaps in between tall and uneven birch trees that glow in the dusk like candlesticks. Amidst that glow, a small clearing stands out, bathed in a white light so bright it makes Luminko's eyes ache. The mossy ground is caught in the grip of winter, turned from its autumn sponginess to a hard packed slab of grey-green stone.

Luminko walks the radius of the clearing with a bowed head, sagging shoulders, stooped back. Each footfall is slow, heavy and, full of hesitation. Thick cords of sand-colored hair fall out from under a dark hood. Bright gold eyes flash out every now and again, downcast and sad. As they near the middle of the clearing, they are especially careful to tend to the bundle of pale yellow fabric in their left hand. A single drop of blood has soaked through, round like a red angry eye glaring up into Luminko's face.

Luminko looks away.

In the center of the clearing, they raise their head. Their dark face is tear-stained, cast in the long shadows of loss. Their typically bright eyes have dimmed, an unmistakable grayness cast over the sunset violet-pink.

As they move their hands, the bundle shifts and a flash of yellow-orange sneaks out. A couple long, red-tipped feathers poke through. Luminko is quick to replace the feathers, quick to cover the small hooked black beak, the white sealed eyelids, the once bright now blood-matted cheek feathers exposing a small round earhole.

The cloth is still as stone. Argo's small body will not move. No matter how much Luminko wishes it to. No matter how much they need their best friend to be alive. No matter how much they've cried.

Reality is so unyielding at times. The best magic in all the land couldn't alter that fact.

Luminko tried.

But the Master Spinners had all agreed. Death is final and wise. She will not be undone.

So, Luminko brought Argo's body here. To the place where, once upon a time, the two met.

It had been Autumn, unseasonably warm. Luminko, still a student of magic then, had been sent into the forest on gathering errands from the master mage of herbology, Filias.

But, en route to the high plains of purple cornflower and blue sagil, Luminko had felt an inkling. gentle but distinct tug of the world's magic felt only by those sensitive to it. Still in the infancy of their study, Luminko didn't know if they had any aptitude for inklings. They didn't know if they had any aptitude for herbology either. But, Master Filias always said: one must try everything in order to find one's place in life.

So, Luminko had taken the inkling as fact and followed it full-out. The pressure pulled this way through the birch trees, pushed that way around the small series of complicated streams, tugged around a boulder, and urged Luminko out into this mossy little spot.

Then, they heard the call. A soft little hip-hip. Barely audible above the cacophonous din of magical creatures in the forest. If Luminko hadn't been standing right under the tree where the poor kula bird was ensnared in a tangle of discarded weaving, they'd certainly never have heard it at all. But, hear the cry Luminko did. And, climbing the ladder-like branches of the birch was easy. The hard part would be coaxing the little yellow and orange bird to accept help. But, Luminko had a plan.

In herbology, there is a certain weed that relaxes the muscles and the mind. It gives a friendly feeling even when there should be none. Familial, even. The herb was on Master Filias' collecting list. The problem was that Luminko hadn't done that collecting yet.

The bird overhead flopped and hip-hipped more desperately. Soft brown eyes surrounded by a patch of pure white skin seemed to beg for help. Bright orange and ember red wings struggled to move. Six-toed little black feet tried to kick and break free. The weaving made as it was of the highest quality knotted cord, only wound tighter around the small feathered body. The little bird's chest rose and fell, panicked.

There was no time to climb back out of the tree, find the herb, prepare it for use, and return to the rescue. No. Luminko had to act now.

With a clench of their jaw, Luminko decided. They'd conjure the herb in an already prepared state and administer it to the poor trapped bird. Then, they'd untangle the bird and let them free. Easy.

Only, Luminko didn't know if they had any aptitude for conjuring herbs, prepared or otherwise. It could be a disaster. The poor thing could die!

The bird's hip-hip turned to a peet-peet! And the repetitions got faster and louder.

There was no time to delay.

Luminko situated themself on a branch with both legs wrapped around the bottom. They clasped their hands over their chest as the description showed hanging in Filias' office. They repeated the incantation, slow and careful not to miss a syllable.

"Ajoy benlien manah manay ohai ohay."

Their pronunciation was clearly imperfect, but it would have to do.

With a flicker and shimmer of reality, a small glass vial appeared in Luminko's hand. A bright green liquid with blue flecks suspended throughout it. Just like the diagram! Luminko popped the little cork off the top and tasted it with the tip of their own black tongue. The flavor was sensational! Floral and sweet, like drinking the nectar straight from a camaroon gord! Delicious!

But what did it do?

Luminko paused and felt their body, prodding their muscles and gut with stiff fingers. No change. That wasn't good, but it wouldn't make things worse. Would it?

The little bird's peet-peet went still. So did their little black scaly feet. And their bright plumage laid down flat against their little body. The brown eye closed, turning into a little upside down smile. So deceptively peaceful.

Luminko's heart ached. It was too late.

An inkling rose up like a struck spring inside Luminko and urged them to administer the tincture anyway.

Right now!

They did.

The little upside down smile of an eyelid became a glossy brown eye again. The feathers ruffled, held out as they should be slightly from the body. The little feet clenched but did not kick. The black beak opened and out came an appreciative little ahrump that Luminko thought sounded a lot like "argo" -- the name of the great Herbologist Master of old.

Luminko made fast work of undoing the weaving then with their foraging blade. Little Argo laid perfectly calm and still. When Luminko broke the last bind, the bird scampered up their arm and perched on their shoulder. Saved.

Luminko smiled, warmth flooding their belly. They didn't protest the bird's presence on their shoulder, figuring the wild animal would fly off as soon as the herbs wore off. But, all the way down the tree, across the clearing, and through the forest as Luminko went about fulfilling Master Filias' list, the bird stayed put. All the while making that happy little "argo" sound.

The two were fast friends ever since that day.

Tears refresh the dried up riverbeds on Luminko's face as pain and regret twists their thick lips into a dark gaping frown. Why hadn't they been able to save Argo in the end? A diminuative redtailed werehawk attack should have been the last thing to end the bird's life. And yet. Luminko peeked into the swaddled cloth. There was their little love, cold as the frozen earth. Argo's still body was so covered in lacerations and blood that it was hard to look at. All the Masters of magic in the world could do nothing to turn back time.

It isn't fair. It isn't right.

Argo should still be alive.

Sobs rattle inside their chest like wind in the high, glowing birch branches.

Luminko wraps the ornate but bloodstained cloth tighter around the small bird's body. They sink to the hard but mossy ground. It crunches and crackles under knees and calves.

The expression on their face changes from sorrow to worry. Gingerly setting the small swaddled bundle in the dip of their lap, Luminko gets out the little shovel engraved with Argo's name. They had it made special for this terrible day. One they never really believed would come. But, here it was.

Luminko started to dig.

The tip of the spade wouldn't get so much as a knuckle's worth of earth moved.

Frozen solid. Like chipping away at a frozen lake or, worse, stone. If Luminko had been smart, they'd have left this special little grave-digger at home along with the jar full of Argo's old feathers. They'd have grabbed the ice-pik and the hammer-wedge from their foraging tools. They'd have come prepared.

But then, that wouldn't have been suited for this pair. Improv was their joint style. The strange magic of flex and flow. Bend and twist. They used what was there, made it work even when the situation felt hopeless.

Luminko's finger touched the top of Argo's head in a habitual gesture of love. Ordinarily, Argo would turn and nip the tip of their finger playfully, saying "yes, me too." Only now the motion was cut short, truncated by the chill of death.

Withdrawing, Luminko stared at the frost bespeckled moss.

What now?

Argo had to be buried here. There was no question about that. All the magic in the world couldn't have pulled Luminko aside from this decision. This was where they had met; it would be where they would part. Luminko's heart would never sit right otherwise.

But the ground was so very frozen. Packed solid. Impenetrable.

Like the earth itself was rejecting Luminko's pathetic attempt at penance.

They hadn't meant to let the werehawk get to Argo. It'd been a complete accident.

It was such a lovely unseasonably warm morning. Luminko had left the window open. Argo sunbathed while eating a breakfast delivered a little earlier than usual. Luminko got absorbed in their weaving a new picnic blanket for Argo and them to enjoy when the spring came. Visions had danced in Luminko's head of the two of them playing "hide in a tree" in their clearing, singing favorite songs and guzzling sweet orange nectar-filled saintberries.

Then, the screech. Argo's weep-da-weep alarm call, seconds too late. The crash of metal and dishes as the werehawk flopped into the small room. Argo's breakfast strewn across the floor. Feathers going this way and that. And the blood...

So much blood for such a small thing.

Luminko barked out a spell and threw the werehawk back out whence the demon had come. The sun crested over the mountain's edge, bringing in the full light of morning. The werehawk shrieked in irritation at the day, and disappeared in the blink of an eye.

Luminko rushed to their side, scooping the fragile body up into shaking hands, but no.

What was done was done.

Argo never got up again.

The memory is a terror-filled nightmare. Luminko pushes it away, unable to bear the guilt.

Tears refresh themselves double-fold, pouring in rivulettes down Luminko's crumpled face. The saline drips down in big fat drops that soak into Argo's burial cloth. The droplets turn to beautiful little ringletts of ice far quicker than is normal.

The truth hits Luminko like a fist in the jaw.

The frozen ground isn't natural, either. Someone's caused this deep frost, made it impossible to bury Argo here in this clearing. But why? Who would do such a thing? Only one person knew of Luminko's plan. After the meeting with the Master Spinners where they confirmed Argo couldn't be saved, Luminko swaddled their tiny body up as fast as fingers could fly. They took off from the university grounds and made it here in half the time it usually took the pair to meander their way to this favored spot. En route, Luminko had passed only one other living soul.

Master Filias.

The same Master Filias who had sent Luminko out gathering the day Argo was found.

There's a lesson here. Luminko knows it. Only, they can't begin to fathom what it could be. What had Master Filias said in passing?

"Death is not cruel, but an efficient teacher. She changes us from the inside out. She opens space where once we had none. Do not shun death, my dear student. Face her full on."

Words of thin comfort, Luminko had thought then. But now, upon revisiting them, they think there must be something more to learn. Something more profound. Something about this frozen over ground.

A sudden inkling pricks at Luminko's mind.

They start, touching the side of their head in shock. It's been ten years since they'd felt one. The last time had been the inkling that led them to Argo and that little hip-hip. The memory is a sharp knife in their heart.

But, painful as it is, Luminko also remembers a spell they'd quite forgot.

It's an incantation in the dead tongue of the old Master Argo's people: the Morage. The spell is said to open space where there is none. No coincidence the spell's description is the same phrasing as Master Filias' sage advice. Luminko's never seen it enacted nor heard the words of the song that one has to sing in order to call the space into existence.

Still, it's worth a try? Right?

If the inkling says so, who is Luminko to say no?

Opening their mouth, the words tumble out like rain from a laden cloud. Fast and without effort. Luminko's reminded of their own absentminded humming, of the song Argo used to mumble while falling asleep. The dips and rises of the melody are familiar already, and Luminko's throat and chest sing them with ease.

All around, colors spring forth that hadn't been there before. The trees in the clearing shed their wintery palor and spring into full color. The moss shakes off the frost, bursting with red and orange, green and powder blue, yellow with hints of soft violet. Patches of dead leaves disappear replaced by tall seed-laden grasses blowing in a warm yet crisp springtime breeze. The air is full of the smell of young flowers and the green sap of new growth forest taking root.

And just overhead, the faintest hip-hip can be heard above the din of busy insects.

Luminko looks up.

There is nothing there but the bright foliage of budding birch trees.

Still, the hip-hip sounds again.

Luminko stands, cradling the cloth in both hands as before. Only now the weight is much lighter. They look down to find the cloth has fallen open. There is no Argo inside. Only the indentation of the small soft body.

In a panic, Luminko crumples the burial cloth and drops it. That unmistakable hip-hip becomes more desperate. Looking this way and that, Luminko calls out.

"Argo!"

"Peet-peet!" Argo alarm-calls back.

Luminko remembers their first meeting, falls silent. Argo's cries fall silent in kind. Luminko returns to the melody of the spell--the one that should open something where there was nothing before. As they sing, they scramble up the birch tree as fast as they can, thinking only: wait for me.

The soft fuzzy leaves brush their face as they ascend. They can't help but think of Argo's feathers when they'd cuddle against Luminko's cheek just before bed. The air fills with a new scent the higher Luminko goes. All around, it is rich, sweet, and slightly grass. They'd know that smell anywhere. It's Argo.

Looking down, Luminko sees that--by magic--their favorite birch tree has been transformed into the shape of a large phoenix-like bird. The yellows are as bright as the sun. The oranges and ember reds flash and burn in the bright winter light. The black beak is a slice of the dark cloudless sky peppered with stars. Each one, a cherished memory. Luminko could never count them all, but each one is precious.

"Where are we going, Argo?" Luminko asks aloud.

Their voice is whipped away by the wind of Argo's flight.

An inkling, however, fills their mind.

The two of them are returning to Argo's home. The place where all the great Master Spinners of old go.

"Where is it?" Luminko asks, knowing Argo can hear their question even without words.

Just like it was before. The two communicated as two species often do, through understanding and intent.

Another inkling fills Luminko's mind.

The place where they're headed is like a clearing, if the universe were a forest. White birch-like trees stand gathered all around the small oblong shape. Each one represents an Arch-Master of magic: one of the original Spinners of the world itself. Among them, on the moss-covered spongy ground, stands Argo. Tall, uneven, proud. Hair like the sun, skin ember red, and eyes as black as the sky and peppered with the living glitter of pure magic.

Up ahead, a wall of thick ice stands between them and whatever lay beyond. Light glows out like fires burn on the other side. Luminko, afraid, cries out in a terror-stricken panic. Their voice is a desperate but quiet "hip-hip," barely heard above the roar of the wind and the singing of Argo's wings. The phoenix-bird burst through the barrier with no resistance at all. What appeared hard, rock-solid was nothing but the illusion of an ice wall.

Just like the mossy ground in the clearing. Luminko thinks. Master Filias knew full well that the great master spinner of old, Argo, had hidden in bird form. Whether Filias or Argo themself had chosen Luminko to look after the Great Master doesn't so much matter to Luminko. What matters is that Argo is alive.

Death was not the finality the other Master Spinners wanted Luminko to believe.

Or, had that been a part of the plot to get them out to the clearing as well?

Did all the Master Spinners know? Stranger yet, was Luminko the only fool who'd ever believed such a magical living thing like the small bright bird of Argo could be merely just a bird? Had no one else been fooled?

"You've arrived," says a voice that is not Argo's and not inside Luminko's mind.

Luminko looks up to see the black, unfamiliar face of an Arch-Master Spinner. Their head is long, their face is wide and flat, and their eyes are rimmed in pure white skin. When they bow slighly, their eyes become the upside-down smiles of a bird at peace.

"On behalf of the whole Collective, I thank you for ensuring their safe return."

Luminko is about to say "your welcome" when the great phoenix-bird of Argo speaks instead.

"What more could I have done? We were remiss without our tenth arch-master."

Luminko starts, turns to look up at Argo's massive black beak.

"Who do you mean?"

"You, silly," Argo says.

The sound of their voice is like dark wine. Miraculous. Rich and heady. Intoxicating.

"I don't think I follow," Luminko says.

"The arch-master gatherer doesn't remember," the dark-faced arch-master says, eyes still pressed into upside down crescent smiles.

Arch Master Gatherer?

Luminko blinks.

Then, the memory returns.

It was Luminko, Arch-Master Gatherer of the great old Collective who got lost first. Once upon a nightmare, they'd been going their merry way humming a made-up ditty. Out of nowhere, a hole opened up in the spongy ground and swallowed them whole. Down their soul plunged through the starry expanse, until finally, they hit solid ground.

Cold, hard, unforgiving ground. Frost bit at their tender soul. Guilt and regret, sorrow and remorse chewed at the edges of their mind like rats in an overgrown nest. Memories were given sacrifice to the rats in order to survive. Bit by bit, Luminko forgot who and what they were.

Left alone in a mossy clearing surrounded by birch trees, Luminko's body hid away. The only body to ever pass by the clearing was Master Filias, who beckoned to Luminko every day.

"Come, study at the magical university!"

When the winter got too cold, Luminko caved and ventured into town. There, they found the impressive castle of University of Magicks. Filias greeted them at the gates and helped them sign up. Then, Luminko swiftly failed all the tests. Not a single pass. The Master Spinners all got together and discussed. There was something there, indeed, but for some reason--it was impossible to know Luminko's aptitude for magic. Still, Filias fought for their acceptance.

And so, it came to pass.

And then, that day in the clearing.

"You were calling to me, not for help!' Luminko finally realizes.

"Yes," Argo confirms.

"Filias knew you'd be there?"

"Only hoped, as that day was the solstice, when the barrier between our worlds is thinnest."

A terrible stab of pain rises up in Luminko's chest. The memory is so fresh, so painful. Still, they force the words out. "What about the werehawk?"

The black-faced arch-master raised their black hand. "Guilty. There are things here that needed tending. You two have had long enough to play human and bird. It was time to get back to work."

Luminko frowns. "You could have been less gruesome about it."

"Would you have gone then, to the clearing? Seeking something?"

Luminko bows their head. "No, I can't say I would have."

"What's done is done," the werehawk Arch-Master says.

Luminko nods. "So, does this mean the hole I opened up with my careless spell--?"

"--is closed and gone?" Argo asks, then sighs. "No, I'm afraid not."

The werehawk puts one strong hand on Luminko's shoulder and the other on Argo's. "The gateway between our worlds is not necessarily a bad thing."

"That may be true, Filias," Argo agrees, "but there is much work to do in order to make it safe."

"Filias?" Luminko starts.

The werehawk winks and laughs. "You didn't think any old human master was so wise, did you? Knowing every step along the way? Always knowing just what to say?"

Luminko hangs their head, sad. "No, I suppose not. I only hoped, for the humans' sake."

Argo brushes up against Luminko in a way that is old and familiar. The soft cuddle of comfort when things are hard. That unspoken reminder of connection, understanding and intent.

"Don't worry. With the gateway open now, we will be able to help them get up to speed."

"They just have a long way to go," Filias adds, sounding stern, like the old human teacher Luminko was fooled into thinking they were.

Luminko nods. "Yes, it's possible. If we three could stay in the human world all those years and not be corrupted, it must be possible to send engery both ways."

"You've already proven it by your return. Which is why the other Arch-Masters are so eager to hear the tale. Come, let's go."

Luminko and Argo nod in unison, and their bodies move together to follow Filias. Their movements are in perfect balance, like companions, human and bird. A shadow of their years in the human world. Luminko lets out a little laugh. The sound is so much like that of a happy bird.

Just as they're about to come into the Arch-Masters massive star-filled chamber, Argo rubs up against Luminko's shoulder. And a happy little "argo" sound fills Luminko's mind, giving them strength to carry on.

A new inkling rises up inside Luminko's mind, replacing the ache of death. And with it, a vision of a world where humans and Arch-Masters live in unison. A world where magic is vibrant and in perfect balance. A world where death is seen for what she truly is. A teacher and a friend. A transition at the end of a long life into greater things.

Death is final, yes, but she is also so much more. She opens the door to other worlds. So while she will not be undone, she can be embraced and revered. Luminko understands now what Filias was trying to say, how Death opens space. Not a space to undo the past, but one in which the past is understood, cherished and loved.

* * *

# *About the Author*

Rei Rosenquist is a non-binary, queer, solo polyamorous writer of speculative fiction and romance.

Always on the move from one place to another, it's hard to know where in the world they're at in this moment. They study pre-veterinary medicine as well as rescue, rehabilitate, and flight train pet parrots in need. They also read tarot on the side for friends and strangers alike.

Their short fiction has appeared in Giganotosaurus, Heart's Kiss Magazine, and Summer Sizzles by Kristine Kathryn Rusch.

# Also by Rei Rosenquist

* * *

**Collections**
From a Broken Angle
Quietly Recovered
The Siblings Grimm
Stars and Dark

* * *

**Dark Run of the Wolves**
A Worthwhile Sacrifice
Visions of Clover

* * *

**Science-Fantasy Shorts**
Agency Returned
Along These Lines
A Rememebered Kind of Dream
Beyond the Collapse
Gone Astray
Mastery
Where Their Bones Lie

* * *

**Stand Alone Fantasy**
The Body Carved

9 798822 418254 1